MARILYN McLAUGHLIN was b[...]
read English and German at Tr[...]
year in Germany researching fairy tales at Phillips Universität.
She returned to Derry in 1975 and has worked there as a teacher,
a researcher on BBC Radio Foyle, and as an illustrator and graphic
designer. Her short stories and poetry have been broadcast on local
radio and published in various newspapers and magazines, and in
1996 she won the Brian Moore Short Story Award. *A Dream
Woke Me* is her first collection of short stories.

a dream woke me
and other stories

Marilyn McLaughlin

THE
BLACKSTAFF
PRESS

BELFAST

• A BLACKSTAFF PRESS PAPERBACK ORIGINAL •

Blackstaff Paperback Originals present new writing, previously
unpublished in Britain and Ireland, at an affordable price.

First published in 1999 by
The Blackstaff Press Limited
3 Galway Park, Dundonald, Belfast BT16 2AN, Northern Ireland
with the assistance of
The Arts Council of Northern Ireland

ARTS
COUNCIL
of Northern Ireland

Marilyn McLaughlin has asserted her right under the
Copyright, Designs and Patents Act 1988 to be identified as
the author of this work.

Typeset by Techniset Typesetters, Newton-le-Willows, Merseyside

Printed in Ireland by ColourBooks Limited

A CIP catalogue record for this book
is available from the British Library.

ISBN 0-85640-644-9

In memory of
Joanne

Contents

A dream woke me

I HAVE TAKEN A WRONG TURNING on my way back to bed with cocoa, and am now stranded on the landing chair, where no one ever sits, except me on lunatic nights like this, when moonlight floods the house in great rippling waves. A dream woke me, and warm cocoa in bed will help me sleep again. But I sit here instead, perverse, warming my hands on the mug, turning my face into this perilous tide of moonlight. It spills and streams and is alive.

I am glad that this landing window is sealed up with layers of paint, or I would open it and swim out into the air. But then of course I would fall straight into the arms of Birdman's tree and be as safe as houses.

It is Birdman's tree that ripples the moonlight, its leaves stirring against the windowpane. I planted it too close to the house. I didn't see the growth in it. Now it is a huge, muscular tree, embracing the house. The surveyor said it was an act of madness to plant a birch just there.

Birdman brought it home in his pocket, from the woods where we'd taken our last walk, before he flew away to be with his precious planes. He'd eased the little thing from the earth so that I'd have it to remember him by. He said that after the war, when we were married, we'd transplant it into our own garden. I just had to look after it while he was gone.

I hated him for going. I told him so, that evening when he brought me home. He didn't have to go. It wasn't his war. But the chance of flying was too strong a rival. I called him Birdman for spite and slammed the living-room door in his face. The pain in my heart started then, as I stared at that blank closed door, willing him to open it, to come back. I heard the click of the big front door as he let himself out. I heard his feet on the gravel outside, leaving me.

Later I found the little birch on the doorstep, its roots as fine as baby hair. He wanted me to have it. I planted it in the shrubbery, without telling anyone. And now its roots are under the walls and its branches envelop the chimneys. It overwhelms the house.

My brother was here this morning with his surveyor friend.

'Lunacy to let it get so big. It'll crack the house open like a nut.' He said that if we cut the tree down now the house will rise, or was it sink? I forget. I didn't know houses could be so restless.

My brother wants me to leave the house, because of my heart, he says. 'The damp will get in. It'll be unhealthy; think of your condition.'

'I've lived here my whole life. You'll not uproot me now,' I said.

The nice polite surveyor didn't know what to do about this, so he withdrew to the car. 'Good for another few years yet,' he called from the safety of the front seat. 'But eventually she'll need a fortune spent on her, or she'll just fall down.'

He was talking about the house. I picture it – like two drowning lovers – the house clasped by the tree, being drawn down, down, down to its ending. I'll be dead before that happens, so I don't care. I can live with a few cracks, a few slipped lintels, with damp.

Birdman didn't come back of course. He never claimed his tree, or my future. Downed in the desert: I pictured, at the time, the spiralling fall of the plane – by night, by moonlight perhaps? Birdman, no more. Gone. Never, never again.

Even now, years later, I repeat this to myself. Some mad part of me still cries out, waking from heart-stopping dreams, still asserts that it's a mistake – he is alive – my mother must have misheard the phone message, or that the phone itself deceived. Take away these words. I will not receive them. My mother rising to answer its ringing as if it is any ordinary call, the cat purring, the coals in the fire shifting, and then the terrible words and us all on our feet, tumult in the living room; and everyone hushing, as the living-room door slowly opens, all by itself, no hand on the handle. No one is there. Only the darkness of the unlit hallway beyond. Father slams the door shut. 'Faulty lock. Have to get it fixed.' That was when the pain in my heart rose up like a wave, and crashed down on itself, scattering foam through every corner of the house.

The living-room door never slips its lock now. It has lost its loose habits and admits no ghosts. That surveying man said the tree has done this: something in the house, I forget what, is slowly tightening. The roots of the tree have invaded the foundations, are pushing, shoving against them.

I should have plucked the tree out, or chopped it down. I should have thrown it away, axed it, poisoned it, rooted it out, long ago. But my head was in the clouds. How was I to know it would grow so big? I couldn't read the future. And I've got used to it being there. The branches tap tap tap against the house; in fierce storms they break themselves against the walls. On summer nights when I leave my bedroom window propped open, the leaves rustle and whisper to me all night long – pillow talk.

The cocoa has gone cold. I'll not sleep tonight. I've had the Camelot dream again, earlier. That's what woke me. It is a good dream. In it I am sailing along a river. The water below me is shallow and clear. My boat is light and likes the shallows. I sail her solo and drink river water and eat berries from overhanging branches. I travel light, without baggage and in my thin frock too. Birdman will keep me warm when I get that far. I've forgotten where he said he would wait, but it's somewhere along the banks of this stream. I'll not overlook his blond and curling hair, or sail by his steady blue regard. I make no effort, and float along quite lazily, down to

Camelot, maintaining only an edge of watchfulness. It will be pleasant to get to Birdman, but it is also pleasant to make the journey.

Raspberries and the dream workshop

'I AM STANDING IN A SMALL ROOM,' she said. 'In front of a mirror. I see that I am covered in blood. The walls are covered in blood, the floor, even the ceiling. I say to my mother "What is happening to me?"'

I know at once what is happening to her.

'Work with this image,' the workshop leader urged – an eminent man; the room was packed.

I say nothing. Men answer quickly, as they always do.

'She's killed someone.'

'Or something ...'

'She's committed some crime ...'

'Out damned spot!'

'She's at war with herself, or someone.'

'Death ...'

'Crime ...'

'This is a very powerful image. Explore the image of blood. Take it further,' the leader says.

I still don't speak up. How can I shout it out aloud from the back of the room with all these people, men and women, to hear. I yearn to speak up, but I am ashamed of what I would say, what all of us here must surely know. These men are giving only their side of the story. I could tell this girl the meaning of her small blood-soaked room. But I cannot speak out. *I cannot offend.* A priest nearby calls out confidently. 'The blood of life – the holy sacrament.'

That night I cannot sleep. I lie awake in my dark bed, chilled at how shame had stopped my mouth. Why was it not to be spoken of, its potency lost to the world? I talked to him about it, but he didn't understand.

'You colluded. It's the way you women want it. There's nothing to stop you speaking up.'

But there is. He can't see it. I can't put it in words for him. He tells me to go to sleep, maybe I'll dream about it.

But I don't sleep, or dream. I lie awake in the darkness, and a memory opens itself to me. I see myself in a garden at an age when the rhubarb leaves topped my head, and I could see through the darkness between their thick red stems to where the hidden thrushes hopped.

Don't touch the rhubarb leaves. There is poison in them.

I never touched the rhubarb leaves, though it would have been nice to feel their bigness. I was standing where the earth was freshly turned over, rich, scented and black.

Don't get your shoes dirty.

The earth was soft below my feet. The sides of red worms glistened where a spadeful had just been turned over. I was bidden to hush, for the robin was near, and a few dirty grubs were dropped on my hand to hold out for the robin to take.

Wash your hands.

I didn't care. And then a radish was pulled for me – the earth roughly wiped off in the palm of my grandfather's huge hand – and the cool round root was given me.

Don't eat that. It's dirty.

I ate it. I was licensed to eat germs by my grandfather's higher authority. He ate dog biscuits. I yearned for one – they were squat and coloured pink, yellow, green, of different shapes. He said I didn't have the teeth for them. That didn't stop the yearning as I stood on the stone floor of the pantry, watching him eat dog biscuits.

On visits to my grandparents, I wore my Sunday best: a frock that buttoned up the back and had a sash to be tied in a bow behind. And I had a cardigan, to be kept on always, because you caught pneumonia at the slightest chill. Grandfather took me to the garden while the big people sat and talked. When he began to scythe around the apple trees he told me to stand back, away from the flashing blade. After a while he forgot about me, and I drifted off alone to where the cinder paths divided beds of fruit bushes.

Don't go off on your own.

I'd been here before, but never alone. The paths were lined with small box hedges but I could push through in places to the stands of gooseberries, currants and, best of all, raspberries.

I plundered first along the line of peas – which was forbidden enough for me not to want to be seen helping myself. I hid behind the plants as I went. Here was the only part of the garden visible from the house, and if they saw me alone in the garden they'd come and take me indoors.

Always stay where you can be seen.

After the peas came currants, red, white and black, in translucent bunches, gleaming like jewels in the leafy shadows, and then the gooseberries, gold or green, smooth or hairy, sharp or sweet, juicy, the skin soft and opening to the tongue.

Don't eat between meals.

And then the raspberries – you had to go deep through the canes for them – large, darkening red, falling easily into the hand, each larger and sweeter than the last.

Make sure there's no grub in the hole.

I always checked. I didn't want to eat grubs. But I'd eat raspberries steadily – there'd always be a bigger, better, juicier one, next, up there, through here, along there; oh look, how many, more, more, more than a girl could eat. I gathered up the skirt of my Sunday frock to make a pouch, and held it with one hand. It was a mostly blue frock, with rings of wigwams and dancing Red Indians around the skirt. Carrying things in your skirt was what girls – princesses and beggar maids – did. Into the lap of my skirt went the raspberries that couldn't fit in my mouth.

You'll make yourself sick.

I found yellow raspberries, pale gold, so ripe they had no substance in my mouth, bursting into sweetness. But the red were my favourite – darkening to a dusky, bruised crimson, loaded with juice, ripe in their forest of pale canes.

I found a corner and hunkered down to feed from the hoarded berries in the lap of my skirt.

Nice girls don't show their knickers.

But I was secure here, invisible, tented over with leafy growth, the air full of golden hovering insects, the mossy stones bright in the afternoon sun. Only birds knew where I was, and they wouldn't tell.

Then a call came from the kitchen door. 'Teatime. Teatime.' I'd have to go. I scooped a last handful of raspberries from my skirt and filled my mouth. I ran along the cinder paths, full of the taste of the juice, and arrived at the kitchen door. The voice was alarmed: 'What have you done to yourself? Look at her.'

I looked down. A calmer voice said, 'It's only raspberry juice.'

The entire front of my skirt was soaked with a spreading red stain, dark over the blue wigwams. I held it up, away from my thighs. I'd nothing to say for myself. I'd been found out, caught in a hundred transgressions, and there for the world to see was the stain – the stain on my skirt, the stain on my face where I blushed with shame. I stood there wordless, small, and without defence. I wept and would not be consoled.

'It's not as bad as all that. It will wash,' they said.

But I knew it would never wash.

Threads

THE GLOBE STANDS IN THE CORNER. It has been there so long that I never look at it. But what he has just told me has jolted me so hard that sitting on this sofa, in my usual place, my usual cushion at my back, I find myself disconnected from my usual self, and my eyes grope from item to item of this room as if by remapping its details I can reach again the long-accustomed familiarity with which I view my world.

I have seldom been so upset. This I have carefully concealed from him. I'll not make his choice any harder by letting him know how loudly the silent *No* with which I've heard his words resonates along my bones. He wants to emigrate. He has come in, my son, grown too tall now for the chairs to hold the whole of him, and told me how he has a chance of promotion, a change of job, a change of continent. He talks of moving out into a wider world, away from the shrunken parochial boundaries of here. And just before he leaves the room he asks me to break the news to his dad. For all he's a man of the world, he's afraid of seeing tears in his father's eyes.

I cross the room to pick up the globe and I place it on the table by the window. I blink at it in the sunlight. It belonged to my husband's childhood and is a faded, dated thing. Countries have changed their names and boundaries, but the pattern of sea, river and mountain stands true. I spin it till my finger rests on and obscures totally my island, my Ireland, his home, and trace the journey he will take out over the faded blue ocean.

I drive north to the headland, where the lough opens into the sea. I always come here to walk and think, to retreat. I came here with my books when I was in college. We did our exams in the September and I studied all summer. I came here then for the silence and the solitude, to concentrate my mind on my books, but today it is myself I wish to study, to understand.

The day is warm and bright. There is no wind, and the harebells stand unruffled on the roadside banks. They are as blue as the sky, as blue as the sea. I release the impatient dog from the car. I let her run. My thoughts run too.

The *Völkerwanderung* – the wandering of the peoples – a word from my half-forgotten studies. How hungry I was then to learn. I gobbled up all I could find of that time between myth and history when Europe came to the boil. Rome crumbled, the Huns on swift horses rode in from the East, the Arabs pressed from the south. Nations, displaced and armed, crossed seas, rivers and mountains, jostling for *Lebensraum* – space to live – but of course my mind is not so sharp now, that was Hitler's word. Still the principle's the same. The need to establish the necessary defensible boundaries – sea, river, mountain – these mapped the *Lebensräume*. Lombards, Franks, Alemanni; allegiances drawn up and dropped; Pope and Holy Roman Emperor securing boundaries by sleight of hand. *Civitate dei* – the City of God on earth, a new world. And threaded through the nations the wayfarings of the Irish monks, *peregrinatio in Christi* – journeying in the service of Christ. They were the warp in the web of Christian Europe, threads of influence crossing in distant places, far from the selvedge.

I sit on my northern rock on the edge of Europe and look east. I will not turn west, to where the sun sets and the Atlantic rules: great, grey and empty. I have settled against a warm rock and am hunkered down on the short grass. The dog sits beside me and watches twitchily. How easily my son gave me the responsibility of breaking the news to his father, and how will I do it? I can't even seem to break it to myself. I watch my thoughts wander forth – a *Gedankenwanderung* – it affords respite.

The dog watches flies, a distant sheep. I watch a toy-sized distant boat draw its wake towards Green-castle. And I think of all the ships that have sailed the narrows between there and the pincer of Magilligan: the military, the mercantile, the missionary and the migrant. I visualise each journeying ship over centuries leaving a visible and permanent wake like a thread. I try to estimate the density of cloth they'd weave. Overhead up in the blue sky a plane passes, tiny, silver, glinting, heading north-west – a shuttle drawing a weft of vapour trail behind. I settle more firmly on my rock. No one will come to disturb me; I can allow my mind to empty like the sky without clouds, like an edgeless space. But the thoughts dart through, crossing and recrossing, interwoven. I let my mind wander and disperse myself. A *diaspora*. I love uncommon words. They are easier to match to mysteries.

It is what my mother used to call a pet day. The sky and sea are equally endless, fathomless, blue, and the cultivated opposing hills on the far side of the lough roll back one behind the other eastwards into another blue distance. Earth, air, water, tending to blue. I feel I can see for ever. On a day like this if I walked further over the headland and turned north I would see Scotland, blue, over the water.

> Speed bonny boat like a bird on the wing
> Over the sea to Skye ...

A song from school days. I neither knew nor cared about the bonny king, who he was or why he journeyed. My attention never reached the rest of the song. It took flight over Skye. I repicture the ranks of heavily grained, dark-brown desks we sat at, each punctuated by a sunken inkwell. Miss White's Primary 7 qualifying girls: becardiganed, socks neatly held up with knotted elastic garters, hair plaited or pinned over to the side with Kirby grips, ink-stained fingers folded on the desks in front of us; we offered up total obedience. We toed the chalked line, and on Friday afternoons we sat in wooden rows and sang:

> Speed bonny boat like a bird on the wing
> Over the sea to Skye ...

My imagination, all by itself, without first raising its hand to ask for permission, would leave the dark-brown, varnish-smelling classroom, its air clotted with pluses and minuses, laboriously looped and blotted joined-up writing, sums filled with workmen digging holes and baths with dripping taps ... My imagination soared instead over the sea to Skye, sliding down some broad wind like a sea bird heedlessly tipping over into a vastness of air, annexing its unbounded blueness for a playing ground, not *Lebensraum*, but space to ... go. You see, my mind has always wandered.

I wandered once, not far, to Germany and back again, rejoicing in the journey home, from Frankfurt to London to Dublin and to Derry, alighting at the bus station, drawing around me like a shawl my well-remembered boundaries of sea, river and mountain – the lough, the Foyle, the Sperrins. Of course my son needs boundaries of his own, even if they do not match mine. If he thinks he needs a bigger space, then go he must.

The ancient Celts centred themselves wherever

they went. They secured defensible boundaries, looking to the north, south, east and west, named their encircling seas, rivers and mountains, and at the centre point, where the lines joining the compass points crossed the land and met, they raised their monuments, picturing out in stone their belongingness in the universe. Celtic monuments matching Newgrange have been found in France. They've left their mark in Czechoslovakia. Celts, moving westwards, centred and recentred themselves. My son has more Celtic blood than me. He'll gain secure boundaries in his new land, and recentre himself. And I'll be one of those boundaries. I'll sit on the eastern selvedge of his new world, my finger on the thread of his life.

A granduncle of mine sailed over many seas. In Valparaíso he nearly drowned, and wrote a letter home to his little sister. Granny showed it to me once. How clearly across all the seas and the disappearing years that man's voice spoke from the pages – gentle, loving, teasing. Nowadays my homesick, seafaring granduncle could simply phone home.

I'll tell my husband tonight. He'll think it's the end of the world. But it won't be.

Aspects

THE WEST – ACOLYTE

Granny was always odd, they said. And that's why they sent me here, because, being odd herself, she doesn't notice oddness in others, and was likely to put up with me better than they could at that time. They hoped, you see, for me to get better, to change back into what they wanted. So it didn't make sense to me, from their point of view, to send me off to stay with someone odd. But then, they don't have much sense. Perhaps they think two oddities cancel each other out. Anyway, the doctor said I needed space free from conflict and confrontation, real or imaginary. I needed time to heal my psychic wounds, real or imaginary. The doctor made it up as he went along. I could tell by his eyes. But they, of course, believe every word spoken by a doctor, lawyer, teacher or anyone at all on TV or Radio 4.

My body, previously a flat, uninhabited plain, was developing a new geography. I didn't like this. I was getting soft zones. I could feel garlands of flesh begin to settle around my waist and shoulders. I hated this. They weighed me down. Mum said I would inherit a full and graceful female figure, and should celebrate. But she would say that, wouldn't she? Look at her. Look at fat Marion.

I didn't like fleshiness. I have the spirit of an acolyte, pure and clean. I don't like sweating and sneezing and blowing your nose and those other horrible things that boys go on about all the time, and this other thing – I was not doing it. Just not. Never. A thing like that would not happen to me. I saw it happen to Marion, all the whisperings and pains that you couldn't say what they were, a hidden contamination. I didn't want to grow up. I would not become a woman if this awful smearing shameful juiciness, this dreadful spreading uncontainable stain, was part of it. And it hadn't happened to me, even though I was older than Marion was when it happened to her. That's because I stopped eating when I began to grow. And it all stopped. I hovered below the crucial body weight (quote from the doctor).

I intended to stay just as I was – I would never have to wear tight clothes, or high heels, or lipstick, or put rollers in my hair, or powder on my face, or be nice to boys, or make conversation. I wouldn't be looked at. That would be the worst, to know that everybody was looking at your bum or your bosom. I could go about being my usual invisible self, just left to do my own things, and never be commented upon, like a fairy at the bottom of the garden. I liked being bone-thin. I felt as if I could fly. There was just some little trick to it that I hadn't found out yet.

But of course they raised a row. The tears, the yelling, the nagging, the pleading, the understanding talks, the persuasion, bribery and corruption: *Think of your mother, think of your father, think of your sister, think of your future, of course you like boys, of course you want to look your best, would you like a trip to the hairdresser, but you would be so pretty if only you'd eat, I made it specially for you ...*

I like my odd Irish granny. She leaves me alone. We used to come here for holidays when I was little. But that was long ago. Then Mum got her job, and for some reason that stopped us going to Ireland, and we went to Marbella or the Algarve or Tuscany, or Orlando. I travelled to Granny's on my own – first time with a ticket round my neck, like a parcel.

The first thing Granny did was take me into the garden. She spends all her time in the garden, even when it's raining. That's how I get so much time to myself. She showed me round the garden. It's like a jungle. I don't know what she does out there all the time. Everything's enormous and all mixed up through each other – in a mess really, but she has it a different way in her head. She explained how the garden lay diagonally to the points of the compass, so that each corner points straight north or south or whatever. She took me to the gateway with an arch over it.

She said, 'And this is the north – and look . . .' She lifted up some big floppy leaves at the foot of the archway and there were big stones underneath – smooth green stones with great big splashes of red on them, as if they were streaked with blood. 'These are my guardian stones,' she said. 'When I first saw them I didn't like them, because of the red on them. But they do no harm here. They keep me safe from the north, like human sacrifice to ward off evil. And look over here ...' She scurried across to another corner, where there were paving stones and a view along the side of the house, over a fence to the sea, very far off or so it seemed. 'The wind howls through here in winter,' she said. 'The west wind from the sea. This is my favourite corner. You can see the sunset from here, beautiful, and on a stormy day the air smells salty. This is where I have my angels.' And she pointed at a layer of stones of all sizes that edged the paving. They were grey, rounded, with a single white line that marked out a circle on each stone.

'When your dad was small, he found one on the beach and said it was an angel because it had a halo. So of course, I just had to have some angels, and after that every time we went to the beach I brought back an angel, because I needed them to guard the west, as many as I could find, because the west can be tricky. The west can be very dangerous. It has the lure of other lands in it, of Tír na nÓg. That's why the old hermits built their stone houses as far west as possible and sat there, praying their heads off. I like to think of this whole western corner of the garden shimmering with angels, all hovering and singing in the air, like a cloud of midges.'

My mother had said to me, privately, getting me ready to come here, that Granny was as mad as a hatter, and she wasn't sure that this was the right place for me, and that if Granny got too strange I must phone home at once and be fetched. All this had made me feel a lot better about going. I decided, standing in Granny's cloud of angels, that I liked it here, and that I would never go home. Granny herself was a bit the way I imagined angels, somewhat shrunken and with a dry powdery skin, gone beyond the juiciness of my mother and Marion, less earthen than ordinary people, her physical substance drained and faded, as if from the right angle, in the right light, she would be edging towards invisibility. This was how I thought of angels – purified out of earthly nature, invisible and able to fly. My flesh was shrinking, my bones were thinning. Absence of food was lightening me.

Granny loved her food, which she ate in strange combinations and at strange hours. She told me to take what I wanted from the cupboard or from the garden, and if she was cooking she made extra for me and put it on a plate. But she never argued about me eating and would give my untouched food to the dogs without comment. I ate some things sometimes, not often, and only things that allowed me to remain light, and grow lighter.

I sometimes helped granny in the garden. In fact I kept myself very much confined to the garden. On this particular day I was helping her pot on some foxglove seedlings, tiny little things.

'They'll not bloom until next year,' she said. 'They need time to get their feet properly under them, just like some people, and then you'd never credit how big they get.'

I dabbled my fingers in compost, tucking in the tiny roots. 'Where will you plant them?'

'They need the right place to suit their nature. They like shade. I think they'll go beside the wall.'

Lifting and sifting handfuls of earth, I found a fragment of seashell. 'Granny, is it far from here to the sea?'

'No. You can walk there.'

'Do you ever go?'

'No. I never go now. Used to, of course. You have to climb some rocks and fences. I'll show you.'

'To go myself?'

'Why not? But take something to eat with you. You'll get hungry if you're away long.' And she pulled some ripened pods from among the rows of pea plants and slipped them into the pocket of my cardigan.

Then she showed me the path to the sea. We went up the road slightly and stopped at a rusty gate. It was a high, barred gate that had to be climbed, but that would be easy; and beyond was an untarred lane running westwards under stunted sycamores.

'It doesn't go all the way, mind,' Granny said. 'It ends at another gate. Just climb it and follow your nose, and you'll be there. Mind you, there's no sand, just rocks.' Granny waved cheerio and then scampered off back along the road to her garden harbour.

Slightly scared, but excited and determined to reach the sea, I climbed over the top bar of the gate and set off along the shadowy lane. The air was full of midges that jigged in the filtered sunlight like dust motes, and bit continuously. I could see why Granny hadn't come this way for years. I plucked a stem of bracken from the ditch and, waving it vigorously about my head to keep the midges off, I traversed the lane, the other gate and, leaving the midges behind, two fields empty of cattle but littered abundantly with cow dung.

I climbed a slight rise and found myself looking down on a pebbly edging to a blue summery sea. I dropped to my knees to conceal my presence: further along, on the shingle, two fox cubs were playing like puppies, dancing about and around each other, playing tug of war with lengths of seaweed. This was the loneliest, most private faraway place I'd ever been in, and I'd found it all by myself. I sat and watched the foxes for about an hour, and began to eat the peas that Granny had stored in my pocket.

I went there every day, all summer. Every day Granny would give me something out of the garden: peas, radishes, tiny carrots, bits of lettuce, and later raspberries, gooseberries, currants of all colours. I took my sketchbook with me and drew. I'd never been happier. Granny didn't care if the clothes flapping loosely on my bony shoulders were filthy. She never said anything about my hair or wanted me to wear lipstick or high-heeled shoes, or to try on jumpers in shops just to see did the colour suit me. Even when she drove into town for messages Granny let me be. She wasn't much tidier herself. The pair of us were a disgrace: Granny all shrunken with age in her Oxfam finery with a hat on, and me all shrunken by something else in my flapping, raggedy jeans.

It was good to be let be, and the weather was kind that summer. I was able to go out and about every day, my pockets full of fruit or sometimes a piece of scone bread lifted from the kitchen table. I explored as much of the rocky coast as I was able to climb over. There were cliffs I had no intention of trying. I didn't want to be an angel yet. My greatest pleasure, though, was to find a good rock close to the surge of the waves and sit there, idly watching the rise and fall of the foam, the dripping of the wet rocks, the pouring of the water, the colours of the waves. And I began to think more and more of mermaids – most often when

I perched somewhere to watch the sun set. I would wedge myself just out of the reach of the water. At that hour, often, the wind would drop, and the swell breathed against the rocks as gently as a sleeping child. Lazy arms of seaweed stirred from below to elbow the surface and sink. I became more and more sure that here, one day, I would see mermaids.

In anticipation I filled my sketchbooks with mermaids – drifting, drowning, floating mermaids. I gave them seaweedy hair and drew currents of water around them and fitted their bodies into this flow. I lavished detail on their tails and hair and gave them all rounded shoulders and breasts and swelling stomachs above their fishy tails, because that was the way I knew they were, full-fleshed, and never weighty because they swam in the water as if they were flying. Anything too slender would be washed away, melted; mermaids had to be rounded to exist. They were like the rounded beach stones, smooth and firm; mermaids for all they swam and were fishy were as solid as the earth. I gathered shells and felt their swelling roundness; I liked to find round stones that fitted my palm and carry them with me, all day. As I wandered I rolled granny's round, pearly green peas on my tongue, palmed one of the small hard apples that had begun to drop from her trees, bit into its bitter flesh.

Some days I didn't go to the shore. I stayed in some green cave in the garden, busy with my mermaids. I brought in handfuls of garden fruit to eat as I drew. The raspberries were quickly over. They stained my pockets red. Granny was mean about the strawberries. She wanted them kept to be eaten at suppertime. I gave in on this. She made such a ceremony of it.

The two of us sat with basins of water, washing and hulling the floating strawberries, and then shared the arduous task of whipping cream with a fork. And then she would set castor sugar in a silver-topped shaker and her best Waterford dishes on a tray with a linen cloth. She liked best to eat the strawberries at sunset, at the rickety folding table at the western corner of the house.

'It's as if somebody had pulled the plug,' she said, 'and all the light just poured down the plughole.'

'It's not like that,' I said. 'There's another land under the water, where the sun goes at night and there's no earth, no rock, no bones, everything is soft and floats.'

Sometimes we sat in the dark and waited for the moon; sometimes the evening grew so quiet I was sure I could hear the sea, even at this distance. Granny once said she thought she could hear the dew falling. I said I thought I could hear the snails sliding through the grass. She said she was going to

get her torch and her brick to murder them before
they got her flowers.

I'll never forget that summer. I began to put on
weight. I didn't mind. I really didn't. I felt a softness grow on me. I became my own body and
allowed myself to flow freely into every corner of
myself. When I breathed in, I breathed right to the
soles of my feet. And when, one evening, alone by
granny's angels, just as the sun set, I felt the warm
blood of womanhood unfold between my legs, I felt
neither contaminated nor ashamed. I felt I flowed
like the tides of the sea, splendidly.

THE EAST – WATCHER

She had the baby sometime in the middle of the
night. Her husband stayed upstairs with her all
the time. I had gone downstairs exhausted, and had
slept on the sofa with a blanket pulled up over my
head. I had meant to rest only for a moment, just to
settle myself, and then to go back up where she
wanted me to help with practical things, with drinks,
towels, keeping the fire alight in the tiny bedroom
hearth.

But I didn't wake until dawn, when I heard his
feet clumping down the uncarpeted stairs. I heard
him fill the kettle in the kitchen. I think he had

forgotten I was in the house. He was startled when I went in.

'Well?' I said.

'She's had it, a little boy. They're sleeping.'

'All well? Everyone safely through?'

'Yes. Lovely. All well. The doctor's pleased. Said she'd be back later. She's an hour gone.' He had a stunned look about him.

'Here, I'll make tea. You rest.'

'There's too much to do – cleaning up –'

'Never you mind, it's my turn now to be doing something. I must have been asleep the whole night.'

He was asleep even before he got the tea drunk. He slept in my place on the sofa. I covered him with the rug. It was cold in there with no fire on. The range in the kitchen still glowed. At least I'd managed that last night – to get it all stoked up, before I'd slept.

I felt disoriented, being awake and up on my feet at that strange grey hour of the day. I thought I'd never in my life been awake and up that early. I drank some tea at the table – two hands on the cup, elbows on the boards of the table – watching the eerie light seep around the room. It was a sort of fading in reverse. Something would loom out of a dark corner at me and then I'd see in a moment that it was a panelled cupboard, or a row of coats on pegs. I hadn't been often in my cousin's house. Her kitchen was unfamiliar to me.

I remembered the one other time I'd been up and awake at this hour. I hadn't thought of it for years. I sipped the tea. That time I'd thought I was pregnant, and then woke in the dark with the terrible pain – it was daylight before it subsided and I climbed back into bed in the greyness of the new day, knowing that there was no baby to take its risk at life. I didn't want that day to be happening. So I pulled the blankets high up over my head, just as I used to when I was a little girl, afraid of wolves in the night. Rolled up in a blanket, I could survive the very worst the world would do.

I finished the tea and rinsed out the cup with tap water. They drew drinking water from a standpipe in their garden. They had great faith in that water. It came from a spring and tasted like fresh cold air with frost in it. They kept the spring water in the kitchen in two enamel buckets with lids on. The buckets stood in the shade on the stone floor and the drinking water never lost its chill. The tap water that roared out at high pressure to bounce into the big crockery sink on its piles of bricks was for washing.

I stood for a while in the shadowy kitchen,

uncertain what to do. He had said there was much to be done yet and I supposed that was upstairs. I did not want to wake mother and child from their first shared sleep in this world. But I was fed up feeling useless. I tiptoed up the stairs to listen at the bedroom door in case someone would be awake, and then I'd go in.

I found a heap of rolled-up sheets tossed on the landing outside the door. They had blood on them. Here was something to do. I would wash the sheets. I brought them into the kitchen and remembered the noise the plumbing would make if I drew off water to soak them. It would waken the dead, let alone the dead tired and the newborn. But the bloodstains needed to be soaked now, in cold water and salt, if they were ever to be taken out of the cloth. I desperately wanted to clean the sheets. They seemed so intimate, so secretive, like evidence of a crime that must not see light of day, or come under the eye of a stranger. I took an old zinc bath from below the dresser, filled it with the sheets, and opened the front door. I had to undo the bolts. I was the first out that day.

But I was not alone. I had just stepped out onto the cobbles when I saw a form in the open gateway to the road. A fox stood there, calmly watching me. We were the only two beings awake in the world. He didn't fear me and I didn't fear him. The baby and mother were safe, all provisions made. For a moment we stared at each other in greeting. Nothing for you here, I told him silently. He moved off slowly, going on to another place.

As I stood by the tap in the garden waiting for the zinc bath to fill, watching the cloth bubble and float and sink as it lost the air in its folds, and watching the gouts of blood begin to float out of the fabric, I looked up and saw that the eastern sky was full of reddened light, and looking back at the house I saw how the partly opened bedroom window flared with its reflection of the dawn.

The silver twisted cord of spring water rising from its earthen source thrummed into the zinc bath, washing away the blood of birth. The sky filled with radiance, the birds spoke to each other in the hedges, my ankles were wet with dew. From the house a thin wail came, distant and small, but recognisable. The baby was calling out to the new day. I turned off the tap and left the sheets to steep. I ran through the grass back to the house, past the road where the fox had stood.

In my bedroom, in my suitcase, wrapped in tissue paper was the blanket I had knitted in rainbow colours for the baby – bright and tuneful colours, like trumpets and drums. I took it to my cousin's room, so that she could have it to wrap her baby in, to keep him safe.

THE SOUTH – MERMAID

*A*nd you, mermaid, sitting on a rock, thighs swelling
under their own weight, softly moulding to the rock,
*in your white swimsuit and rubber cap, feeling the
summer rain begin to drip drop on your shoulders,
rivuleting down your back and upper arms until you are
all wet just from sitting on a rock, without going near the
water at all. You are waiting for the rain to stop before
going into the sea. You do not mind the cold. It never has
alarmed you and you wait calmly mottling in the chill for
the rain to stop. Then down over the rippled, worm-casty
sand you go, into the seaweedy water. Bladderwrack and
waves washing as one over your shoulders as toes
crunching crabs you wade deeper into the swelling rollers
that lift and sweep you on, until in deep water you swim
like a competent elephant, untiring and without splashing,
buoyant in the greeny deep water, hovering above the sea-
wrack-tendriled forests that sway below you in the
currents that lift and beguile you. And corkwise and
unsinkable in your ample white bathing costume you
swim once up, once down the bay and then emerge,
gorgeously dripping and at a steady untired pace over the
razor shells, cockles and baby mussels mauve like tiny*

dead fingernails and up to the soft sand where lie a towel,
rolled, sandals side by side with stockings rolled and all
your other things in a basket with biscuits, and as you
towel your thighs you look back over the depth of sand to
the lowering sea that rolled you.

I have swum in the sea softened by sun to a liquor warm as blood. My hair is all thickened with salt. I don't wash it away. I let it tangle and enjoy the luxurious knotting. I am trolloping about the place, knickerless in an old kaftan that is frayed at the hem. I eat crisps and chocolate. I am putting on weight and burning in the sun, crisp and brownly crusted. I am a bad mother, most often found on a sun lounger at the bottom of the garden, where the fairies are complaining of the heat, and the petunias in pots go unwatered. Summer is drying to dust. My skin at this stage of life is wrinkled and unelastic, not hugging me so tight and firm as once it did. I hated being young.

The white cat is seeking coolness in the shadow, on the wet concrete where I spilled water, under my chair. He does not settle. There is the lightest of breezes, the gentlest finger playing with the hair by my ear, the water in the egg crock shivers, rocking its blue circle of sky. Midsummer day, and the sun stands at its greatest height. The dog pants, but will not leave me. I have left off my shoes, my bare toes curl like pink buds in the warmth, but I don't think they'll grow into anything other than toes. My hands feel the heat, on their backs, scorching more intense than anywhere else – is the skin there thinner, more used? The pot plants in their pots are almost still, one leaf moving here and there as if breathing. The dog clicks by, toenails on concrete. She wants to be cool but still she will not leave me. I know how it is for the plants, leaves outstretched, suspended in warm still air, garnering heat and the living sunshine, being and growing, all done so quietly in an impenetrable green, sun-shot silence.

Even though I know my toes cannot bud I feel some photosynthesis occur when I steep in sunshine. A spreading laziness permits itself so that petunia-like I can let my sap run upwards, from cell to cell, to my softened surface and allow myself by chemical, sun-led magic to become some other form of me – less strained, less stretched, less anxious.

The graciousness of successive summer evenings long drawn out to the elevenish going down of the sun, a fiery ball among the trees, has been punctured by cloudy weather, unkind to the skin, bringing shivers and goosepimples and taking away the joyousness of the overheated flowers – so that those that bloomed so willingly and doubled, tripled, quadrupled themselves in weeks of unusual warmth are all spread out, with tropical abandon, to a grey sky. The sun has grown shy again.

'Was that our summer do you think?'

'Wasn't it lovely?'

'I could be doing with weather like that all the time.'

But the old women have sat inside and grumbled, begrudging the heat because they do not allow themselves to be flowerlike and, abandoning all caution, to release rivers of pollen upon this opulent air, opening, unfolding, facing upwards to the sun, dozing in its rays, neglectful of household things, sweating, having warm hands, burning wrists, from resting them in the sun on the sill at the open window.

June, July and August, the summer unrolls its litany of sun-warmed days – the sunlight moving around the house, fingering each room in turn, counting the pieces of furniture, trailing fingers of light along the rugs, the walls, and outside in the garden, leaning around the corners of the house to check the compass points, so that hourly, sundial-wise, I know which shadows cross the lawn to cool me like a tide of airiness that finds me, beached in the sun's rays, overwarm, immobilised. I am delivered by the merciful and sober evening light, grey and greying, reminding me of advancing darkness, that all ends and this dizzying vegetative ascent to the sun tumbles finally. The nasturtiums are seeding. The rowans, early, are berried like bold girls in lipstick, reddened and flaunting. I am full of summer, juicy, rich and ripe.

I am one of those over-rounded matrons in shorts and skimpy T-shirt, showing bra straps. I remember a friend who died young and never knew this amplitude of flesh and how it marks down a woman's spirit firmly to the ground and fleshy things, so that the lovely rounded weightiness of spreading hips slows the gait to a luxurious amble, slow-moving and glorious. A middle-aged woman walks less often on air; less buoyant she scoops more often deeply downward into the currents of life where, as flesh gathers on her bones, so gather also in the depths, silts and drifts of fallen things. Downed but not down-hearted, she views all degrees of murkiness that lie below. There is rich nourishment along the lower contours of the sea bed where the heavier-limbed creatures float and dance slowly in the warm water, somersaulting in slow motion, sure of what they do, and unhurried because down here they are doing just what they want and are not subject to vagaries of wind and wave; we are more out of the eyes of the world and into ourselves, less paralysed by mirrors.

THE NORTH – MARINER

The rain comes from the north, driven by the gusting wind in sheets made visible by the shadow of the winter beeches beyond the road. Skirts of rain, fluttered, tangled, ragged – rain fugitive over the fields, whipped over the crest of Rosemount, spilt onto the envalleyed city, thrown against the opposing ranks of hilltops: Kilfennan, Altnagelvin, Gobnascale. I try to picture the miles of land and sea this winter gale traversed to end up here, venting its spite. I do not like the north.

But this north-facing window where my desk stands gives a good steady light for drawing by. I can see the path of my inked nib clearly. This is where I work best, facing out into the teeth of the gale, though this aspect does make me feel lonely, peeled of comfort. I am poised at this northerly corner of the house, like some mythic mariner at the forward tip of his boat, heading northwards into unknown waters: cold, storm-tossed, iceberged, with dragons coiling greyly in the depths below the hull. The light at this window is like the snowlight, cold, precise, that floods the house when the ground and roofs around are all whited out. I love that clarity. Snowlight is surgically precise.

I have on my desk an old drawing, found by chance where it had been abandoned years ago on top of a bookcase. It had caught the sun. It was an original, left out of its file for some reason, and whatever pen I had used had been filled with ink that faded in sunlight. The drawing was bleached from its original sparkling black and white to brown spidery lines on yellowed paper. I had been doubly careless. It troubles me. I place the sun-damaged drawing on top of the work in progress, which is well in hand, neatly pinned out on its board, pencilled in, waiting for the pen. I examine the faded lines and hatchings of the old drawing. It was not meant to disappear into thin air like this. A drawing on sand, a quick sketch for notation, a diagram on a blackboard, all these were footprints in the snow, destined to be lost. But this drawing had been a final statement, a committed black line on paper – something that is so challenging that its commission, in the moment of setting pen to paper, can paralyse the intention, for black ink on white paper does not compromise.

It was my own fault. I had not checked the ink for fastness, the fugitive pigment had taken me unawares and fled. I study the drawing. When I come across something that I once worked on with concentration it usually brings back all the circumstances of its making, as if they had somehow been stitched into the shadings of the pen: the time of day, my mood, the weather, the interrupting phone call. But I can't remember making this drawing. The brown of the line and the yellowing of the paper converge to the same tone. Another fall of sunlight would leave the page a uniform blank again. I feel sad, flooded with something cold, but not unbearably painful, like the north wind blowing over my heart. I slip the drawing under all the pieces of paper, references, sketches that lie on my desk.

I pick up my pen, feel its weight in the crook of my thumb. I am commissioned to do drawings for a book of fairy tales. I am working the final inking. Black-and-white arabesques dance across the page, placed by rhythm rather than by eye. The stylus skips on the paper with a life of its own.

I am alone. The emptied house stretches below and behind me. The south-facing rooms where the children played when they were young are some-times full of sunlight at this hour, even in wintertime. It makes carnival, dramatically jumbling shadows and highlights, exploding the coloured cushions and rugs into an ever-louder, more excited patterning of blue and gold and red. The colours in those rooms, at this hour, could deafen you, and were joyous.

Here in this northerly room, with my door closed to the sunlight, which has its own agenda, in the diffused clear light from my window, I draw. My fine black line finds out the curves and softnesses, the angles, structures, textures. It snips like a surgeon's knife into the white paper, uncovering tone, aspect, the nature of the things I am drawing. Stroke by considered stroke, I slowly build a real little world, bringing it forth out of the play of light made black and white. I always feel that even the most inanimate object in my drawing tells me about itself as I find out, penwise, how it is made.

This is a drawing with trees and pebbles, and a little girl on a pathway, afraid. Even the hem of her coat looks disturbed; the toadstools at the side of the road lean anxiously forward, as if listening like her for whatever lies ahead. All is spotlit, dramatically figured forth by the fall of light through an opening in the trees.

I stop drawing, and listen. The rain spatters against the glass, but louder still is the unperturbed silence of the house. I listen to the deep, deep silence, my mind floats on it, as if on water. If I can hush myself enough, I can match this silence and melt into it, a pure, untroubled deep silence, out of which I look around at the house, at its furniture and the things that sit about – things that I will pick up in a moment, and things that will lie like tidal detritus: his things and the children's things. I am floating silently in a pool of silence that embalms a life, and soaks into me, so that I too could be embalmed. But I resist this. I'm not dead yet – just alone with all these things, the used and the unused, and my work.

Sometimes in the silence of the house I play with memories, like putting on favourite records. I hear again the voices, the arguments, the thumping of feet on the stairs, the intolerable music they listened to. Time concertinas, playing its own grotesque music, years seem like days. My faded ghosts, my shadows challenge the silence, but the silence wins. It remains. But I'll not sink down and in, motionless, and be embalmed. I feel a sharp melancholy, a loneliness – but I know it now for a part of life, not an affront. I can use this current of unpainful sorrowing to swim upwards to the surface of the silence and balance my life raft there, or, rather, a little sharp-prowed boat that will proudly grope round northwards and set sail for the land of icebergs and clear white light. To get there I shall need a wind from the south. I heft my pen in my hand.

Oh Susannah

SUSANNAH WAS A LARGE AND LAZY LADY. She wore an air of sleepy comfort and was not at all a noticing sort of person. She barely noticed where the children left their toys and dirty socks or where the cat left her kittens. She went easily through life.

She had weathered early widowhood with tea and

buns, and was comfortably off. Her friends came often, dropping in always, never invited. Susannah never organised anything. She would laugh and greet them, always pleased and never busy. She would put the kettle on and get out sticky gooey things to eat: baked or bought, it was all the same to her. They would clear a layer of cardigans and books from the armchairs in the big bay window and sit in the sun.

'Help yourself,' Susannah would say, and helping herself she would kick off her shoes and draw her plump feet up under her. She would admit with a sleepy smile that she had no news.

'But I don't mind,' she would say. 'Tell me yours.' For she loved listening. She heard it all, without criticism or advice, and laughed at the funny bits. Nothing shocked her, nothing won condemnation from her. Her friends loved her. She was like a comfortable old chair, softly easing all aches and pains. Her friends had divorces and desperate love affairs, and brought Susannah their tales of pain and triumph. One friend once brought her brother Ivor, an uneasy batchelor. He padded around in Susannah's wake and helped put pastries on a plate. He said little, but his eyes never left Susannah.

'Piggy little eyes,' Susannah's friend Cissie said to Susannah's friend Sarah. But that was behind everybody's back. He came again, alone, to mend

Susannah's broken gate, and walked her children and her dog. Susannah shrugged and said she didn't mind if it made him happy. She didn't mind when he sought to know her better. But he floundered on her perplexing indolence. 'I'd have to think about it,' she said, and shrugged, when he suggested a candlelit dinner for two. And while she thought – she took her time in everything – he kept on dropping around until they both got used to things being just as they were. Or at least Susannah did.

She got so used to him coming around that she barely noticed when he stopped. 'But where has Ivor been?' she asked.

'Spending time with Annabel. Annabel has designs on him. A shame. I thought one time that you and he –'

'Why, so did I,' Susannah said, pondering.

She found she noticed Ivor now by his absence, which was somehow more noticeable than his presence. He called to fix her gate again. He was a noticing sort of man, and driving by on his way to Annabel's he had seen its reassumed droop.

Susannah greeted him with a new attentiveness. He noticed this, and venturing his hand upon the softness of her shoulders, as they sat among the teacups and chocolate buns, he found himself rewarded with the cosy, sugary kiss that he had pined for.

Annabel, being an extremely noticing sort of woman, soon perceived an absent-mindedness in Ivor and, tracing his erring thoughts to Susannah's door, arrived there one day all unexpected, her tap-tap-tapping at the door awakening Susannah from an armchair doze and disturbing the cats, who all sat up and pointed their ears. Susannah's usual callers just opened the door and came on in, so she knew this was no ordinary visitor. Blinking away her sleepiness, she buttoned the top buttons of her blouse and considered for a moment clearing the muddled ironing from the sofa, but the tap-tap-tapping grew more imperative.

'Oh Susannah,' Annabel said, when the door opened. 'If it had been anyone else, I'd have thought you were out, it took you so long to come to the door, but I know you never go anywhere.'

'So nice to see you, Annabel. This is a surprise. You must take me as you find me.'

For even Susannah noticed Annabel eyeing the chaos of her home. Annabel had no time for Susannah. She considered her a slovenly person and feared it was somehow catching.

'My dear,' she said. 'How homely, and comfortable; but where will I sit?'

Susannah moved a washing basket from a chair and offered tea.

'No, no. I'm on a diet.' Annabel sat down on the edge of a chair, flinching as a cat jumped in behind her. 'I haven't seen you for so long,' she said. 'I was wondering how you are, and really Susannah, I'm surprised to see you still haven't picked yourself up. There's no point shutting yourself away, closing out life. Look at me: I was shattered when Hugh left me – absolutely shattered – but I didn't let myself go. I took control of my life. I got out and about, did things, got a little job, built up my confidence. I've made my life be just as I want it. And what I want I get – be it job, first prize in flower arranging, or man.' She gave an ominous emphasis to this last word that went totally unnoticed by Susannah. Annabel, sure she had made herself clear, rose and, glaring at the cat in the chair, brushed hairs off her neatly pleated skirt. 'Well, I won't keep you back from your ironing,' she said, and left.

Susannah, making no connections, never asking why Annabel had called, quite missing the gauntlet that had been thrown down, pondered only some of Annabel's words. Was life passing her by? Was there more to be had that she'd somehow not noticed?

She joined a crochet circle. The gossip was good. She progressed to an occasional night out with new friends. Someone suggested she try a night class – learn typing. It was fun. She lost weight, fell into a nice little job, and was not always in when Ivor dropped round, and he, at a loose end, married Annabel.

Susannah minded slightly. She was a little hurt, but she'd not miss him much. 'And he had such piggy little eyes,' Cissie said, this time to Susannah's face. 'And anyone careless enough to get himself married by Annabel deserves all he gets.'

Susannah laughed. She was a student now, her house was full of books and papers, the ironing still not done. Her friends called round to talk, and Susannah, more wakeful now, had news to share.

One day, months later, Susannah's garden gate fell off its hinge at her touch and, late for a bus, she wondered for a moment what it was the crooked gate reminded her of. Then she rushed on, and there was Ivor at the library. He did not recognise her, then: 'Susannah! You do look well. Well, well, well –'

She smiled, not in her old slow way that he remembered.

'I have missed you,' he said. And then unguardedly – for she had always been so undemanding, unremarking, that all around her had dropped guard – he said, not meaning to, 'Can I come back?'

Her regard was unrewarding.

'To see you,' he stumbled on, 'some evening – I miss the way we used to be.' But now he knew he had missed his mark, for Susannah, instead of laughing at him in her old lazy, careless way, was looking at him silently, guardedly.

'I didn't really mean to marry Annabel,' he said.

'But Ivor, dear,' Susannah spoke at last. 'It's much too late to mind or mend.' And then she left, the decisive tap-tap-tapping of her high heels crossing the library floor and disappearing through the door.

And Ivor, uneasy husband, had to agree.

Besieged

SHE BROUGHT THE HEAVY GLASS JUG of lemonade to the kitchen table. Then she fetched a tray and opened the yellow linen press to find a tray cloth. The scent of honey from the combs on the top shelf spilled around her as she fingered through the piles of starched linen – napkins, guest towels, tablecloths – and here was a tray cloth, stiffened, folded. Then she lined up glasses for the lemonade, small ones for the nieces and nephews, with a spoonful of sugar in each because last time they'd had her lemonade they'd made faces at its bitterness and not drunk it. She counted out forks and matching plates for the apple tart and then, elbowing open the latch on the kitchen door, she carried the loaded tray out into the glare of sunshine.

She brought it round to the front of the house and set it down by the rug on the grass. She looked around the big countrified garden, eyes screwed up against the glare. The children were scattered, culling daisies and other minor treasures.

'I've found a seashell,' one shouted, 'in the *grass*. How did it get there?'

A sister-in-law dozed in one of the deck chairs. Nearby stood an empty tent, put up in order to give the children somewhere to play out of the sun. Its flaps and strings hung motionless in the heat. The rug and tent and deck chairs marked out a little island settlement in the middle of the untidy surge of lawn. The other woman stirred, lazy, yawning, and blinked around.

'Oh, lemonade! Lovely,' she said. 'I'm parched.'

'Where is everybody?' the aunt asked.

'Gone for a walk, I think. I stayed to watch the children.'

'I only see three of them.'

'The boys are probably in the orchard. You know boys.'

'I'll go and find them. They'll be getting too hot.'

In the orchard she found the boys throwing hard little windfalls out into the road.

'You mustn't throw things,' she said, knowing they would pay her no attention. 'Come for lemonade.'

'But they were throwing stones,' one said.

'Who were throwing stones?'

'The boys in the road – outside.'

'Well you must ignore those boys. They're from the estate and they don't know any better. Don't have anything to do with them.'

'They were breaking through a hole in the hedge. They wanted to get apples,' the boy protested.

'If they come back, your grandfather will deal with them. You must leave those boys alone.'

The children darted away ahead of her, impatient of being scolded, racing for the lawn.

The grown-ups had returned and were gathered

around the tray, some on the rug, some on cushions thrown down on the grass. They were a noisy collection of brothers and sisters, wives and children, sorting themselves out with plates and forks, glasses, sunhats. She joined them, sitting down on a corner of the rug, drawing her feet up under her, tucking them away from the grass. She was glad to insert her silence unnoticed into their rowdiness. She sipped at her glass of lemonade. It stung her throat.

The boys were recounting the battle of the orchard hedge. One of the girls, leaning back tired against her mother's side, asked peevishly, 'Why do they try to get our apples?'

'They're rotten apples anyway,' one boy shouted.

'They're cooking apples, for apple tarts,' his mother corrected him.

But the girl persisted. 'But they're not their apples; they've no right to get them. Why do they keep doing what they're not supposed to?'

'Because they're not good, well-brought-up children like you,' her mother said. 'Now eat up your apple tart.'

The girl was content, happy to feel superior to the loud-voiced, jumping boys on the road outside. She counted out the cloves she had taken from the apple tart. 'Tinker, tailor, soldier, sailor, rich man...' The girls played this game to find out who they would marry, the boys to find out who they would become.

The aunt smiled. She had played that game as a girl. But she had never married. She had had her chance of course, but knew where her duty lay. She had said, 'No,' added 'thank you,' and had come home to keep house for her ageing parents. She had done it well too – impeccably – counting out the tray cloths, brushing the crumbs off the tea table with a little silver-handled brush and pan, marking out the hours with daily tasks, the weeks with visits to church. It had been an unchanging life, protected by custom, walled in as a garden is walled in.

Only once had she faltered. What brought that to mind now? She never thought of that time – so very long ago. She let herself think of it now, touching it lightly in her mind as if to show herself how little it mattered. She had been standing in the scullery at the window, washing dishes with her sister. She had tried to explain. She had said: 'Sometimes I hear voices.'

'Probably boys in the garden, after apples,' her sister had said.

'No, no . . .' she had said, her hands stilled in the dishwater. 'They wouldn't say such things' – words like ravening birds, hook-clawed, dagger-billed, swooping, savaging, tearing at all her certainties, nearly all the time now, she couldn't bear it. She had closed her eyes to absent herself from a place of pain, and had not known that she had flung the basin of hot water onto the stone floor, and that she was screaming, screaming, screaming . . .

Calm and order reasserted themselves – because these were what mattered. You made and mended your life to that end. You disciplined and trained your thoughts as you would children, pointing them in the right direction. In the end the howling words fell silent, and she found her way back to safety, secured by manners and custom. She absolved herself from that broken time in her life. Prayer and routine removed it. She held her head high again and did what was needed around the house.

She had to rise from her corner on the rug. The visitors were going now. The sunlight had left the lawn and the evening was far advanced. Cardigans were called for, kisses exchanged, farewells made. She waved from the gate and then went in to settle her parents in the living room. She switched on the wireless to cover the silence.

It was almost dark when she came back to the lawn to tidy up. She left this as late as she could in order to eke out the pleasures of the afternoon. She lifted the cushions and folded the rug and the deck chairs. She left the tent standing for another day. They were in for a heatwave. She'd have to watch the drinking water. Sometimes the well ran dry.

She was retrieving a last, rolled-away empty glass, which had a handful of drying dandelion heads stuffed into it, when she heard through the almost darkness the clear lift of boys' voices on the road beyond. She fancied she could hear the steady tramp of their feet on the tarmac, even at a distance. Sound carried in the hushed twilight. It must be the boys who had passed by earlier, returning from wherever their adventures had taken them. Their incomprehensible hoots and whistles rose like distant war cries.

She went into the house and pulled the door tight. She switched on lights and drew curtains against the night. The yells of the boys on the road grew louder as they approached the orchard. They leaped and cavorted out on the dark roadway.

She would warm the milk for supper and put the cat out. She would set the porridge to soak for the morning, and get out a tray and a tray cloth and mugs for cocoa. Nothing would change.

Bogman

THE LANEWAY WAS FULL OF SUNLIGHT, gathered up and tossed about in handfuls by the leaves – the new leaves, unmarked and glowing in their greenness. The agitation of the breeze through all the depth of greenery was thorough, down to the tiniest celandine rocking and trembling inches above the earth. It was all excitement along that laneway.

Just past a ruined house, its tumbled walls overcome by a flood of waist-high briars, was the river.

She often came here, where the laneway ended. There was no ford, no line of stepping stones, no lifting up and continuing of the pathway on the other bank. It simply ended. Perhaps it had been made, many years ago, to bring cattle to drink. Crumbling banks and ragged fences closed off the river bank on either side. She was left only with the narrow, gravelly spill that marked the meeting of the laneway with the water. It was a busy little river, shallow and stony, the water noisily hopping from rock to rock, and coloured brown and sparkling gold by the bog it had come from. The bog was never too far away, in this country. Even here, where the trees and hedgerows grew thick and sheltering, this splashing dancing water brought with it the cold peaty air of the hilltop – the abandoned land, given over to sheep and hares, where no tree grew and the wind shaved the heather close to the ground.

It was Danny had wanted to buy the house up there. They had driven up on a day much like this – the best sort of day on which to visit the high country. She'd gone to please him, not saying what she thought about living so high up – and her feelings did not change when she saw the place. Danny had been very keen. The clear air unfolded miles of countryside below them – fields threaded by roads from horizon to horizon, laid out for their inspection like a map. They could have been looking from an aeroplane.

'It's very beautiful today,' she'd said. 'But what about the winter? I bet the cloud comes down all around here. It's so high up.'

'But that would be wonderful,' Danny had said. 'Like living in the sky.'

'But it's so remote.'

'It's what I need. Listen to that silence. I'll write here, I'll mark essays. I'll prepare lectures on the journey to work. It'll be perfect.'

The house had at one time been a home, and then been renovated as a summer cottage, and was now for sale. It crouched low and long, inserted as best it could be into a shallow fold of the land. But there could not be much shelter. The wind over the hilltop would pounce on it in winter. Nothing grew around it. The ground was too stony, too near the bone. Great sheets of grey rock protruded and made the floor for the street in front of the cottage.

'This is fantastic, fantastic,' Danny kept saying. And for love of him she didn't speak her thoughts. This was not where she wanted to start married life. This high loneliness was not for her.

They drove down the mountainside, Danny full of

enthusiasm. She relied on it waning as it so often did. She'd made arrangements to view one other place, on the outskirts of the village not far from her sister's home. They'd look at every other option before deciding.

The house in the valley was wrapped around in a radiance of summer growth. Cows looked over the fence into the back garden where fruit trees grew. Danny, always open to everything that came his way, liked this house too, found out its good points, but thought that it would cost too much, that it was not a house for people starting out, that it was a house for settled people, who had shaped their lives.

'It's a house with middle-aged spread,' he said, 'like your mum, very cosy and knowable.'

She laughed, loving him for the way he explained things. Home would be wherever they were together.

And so they moved into the mountain house. Everyone had objections, in the way people do. She shrugged and laughed and concentrated on Danny's pleasure in the place. On the rare bright mornings when the wind lay down and rested under a clear sky he would eat breakfast sitting on the stone in front of the house, watching the buzzard that lived on the next hilltop, listening to the curlews, smelling the distant sea on the air. She would join him, lean her head on his shoulder, and feel content.

'This is it,' he said. 'Freedom, perfect freedom to be ourselves.'

He said a lot more. He was a man of fine theories – one tumbling after the heels of another, all fiery and exciting, world-challenging. He drew people to him, even to the lonely height where he had chosen to live. The little house was full to the late hours of the night with talk, laughter, debate. And through it all he was carefree – careless of what people thought, careless of the past, careless of the future, careless of everything but his own fine, unpolluted view of the world – which could at times be just as chilling as the winds that scoured the little cottage.

He couldn't understand why she was upset about Helen. And she couldn't understand why he couldn't understand. They had been living in the cottage for a couple of years. She had made it as cosy as she knew how, and had got used to passing her days in this high lonely place. Danny had recently taken a part-time lecturing job, which still left him time for his writing. He was slowly, slowly beginning to make a name for himself. Helen was one of his students.

'But you can't, you can't have her to live here.'

'Why not?' he argued, furious at finding himself thwarted in something that to him seemed all reasonableness. 'She's had a really hard time at home. Her parents have practically thrown her out. She needs somewhere to rest up – to sort herself out. She needs a steady base.'

'But this is my home, not a shelter for runaway children.'

'You're incredibly, unbelievably selfish,' he snapped.

She couldn't bear to disappoint him. She was standing by one of the small, deep-set windows that gave a view of a bank of wet heather topped by a tumbled stone wall darkened almost to blackness in the rain. She began to cry. And then Danny called her manipulative, and grabbing an oilskin from the nail by the door, slammed out into the driving rain.

She remembered Helen only too well from among the many visiting faces that Danny drew around him. Dark, narrow, hawklike, Helen hung on Danny's every word. Her dark eyes followed his every movement. This girl would be a most satisfying pupil, but was dangerously greedy. And because jealousy was dismissed from Danny's universe, Danny's wife could never admit her fear. It did not fit with the wide open spaces of love and trust that he demanded.

'You're so special,' he had said to her one night while the storm blew outside, and for once they were alone by the fire. 'You give me absolute love. I'm honoured by that.' She had flushed with pleasure, entranced by his words. He talked on, almost as in a reverie. 'Your love for me is like a great open space – all accepting, nothing darkens or impedes it. You take me as I am and make me myself. Your love is all around me like the wind, like the air, like the sky...just existing, pure and free. You don't know how much it means to me to be loved this way. Your love lets me live and breathe.' Danny was good with words.

And so she continued to be the air that Danny breathed, the space and distances he needed, and consented to Helen coming to live with them. There was no closeness between her and Helen, and she never lost her distrust of the girl's undeclared motives. So she couldn't understand why she was so shattered, returning early one day from a visit to her sister's house, to find Helen starting up out of Danny's bed, pulling a sheet around her and scuttling away, leaving her to face Danny, who for once had nothing to say.

At last she said, 'I knew this would happen. I knew it was what she wanted.'

'But it means nothing – absolutely nothing.' Danny was putting his clothes on, beginning to regain his self-assurance. 'Don't you know how little it means? It doesn't change a thing between you and me. It's nothing...just nothing. Our love, yours and mine...'

He was not apologising, not searching for excuses, not sorry or guilty. He was just explaining things that were to him self-evident – reasonable. 'What's the matter?' he asked, when she flinched away from his embrace.

She was speechless. She couldn't even stay in the room with him.

She took refuge in the kitchen, mindlessly chopping quantities of vegetables that she was later to throw out. Her thoughts whirled. There was no movement from the other rooms. Helen had gone. There was no guessing what her feelings were and she could picture only too clearly what Danny felt: a sense of mild injury over her unreasonableness which he would seek to persuade her darkened and diminished her love for him. Well, her love for him was her property, shaped by her needs, and not shaped and made by him alone. Love! He talked so much of love. He filled his poems with love. Words, words, words. And what of Helen, whom he dismissed as 'nothing'? How could he diminish a person to nothing? Her love could not flow on around and past this thing. She could not, like a rising sea, encompass this. The tide of her love turned.

She left him. He came after her, seeking her out in her new home in the valley, to plead for her return. 'You are my muse. I don't exist alone.' They walked along the laneway lined with leaves and flowers, lush with moss. He spoke of love. She listened and was unmoved. She thought of the garden she had made around her new home. It was a sheltered place, held as in the palm of a hand by high hedges. Her home was steeped in warm light, her horizons were narrowed and cut down to the earth at her feet, where the seeds she had planted were just beginning to grow.

'I can't go back to loving you,' she told him. 'Your love is too cold and wide and large. I'm not able for it. It's not warmth you want. And that's all I want to give.'

She never heard from him again. Perhaps the cold-eyed Helen had provided him with what he needed. She heard of him, of course. He became well known. She was aware of that as if at a great distance. Her life lay in other paths now – the little paths that were invisible from mountaintops.

She often wandered down the laneway if she had time spare, and stood on the gravel sniffing the scent of bog air carried on the water. It did not make her sad.

The sewing box

M Y HERO AUNTS, dimmed by the sunlit garden air to honey-coloured distant figures, sailed the tartan rug across the lawn through all my bee-stung, pollen-scented childhood afternoons. They read, gossiped, dozed, and sent the two of us off to hunt for dandelion clocks, or a stone with a stripe in it, or an empty snail shell. It was a game they'd invented. We roamed the wilder edges of the garden and when we returned, triumphant, one or other of them would put down a book and show us how to string fallen rhododendrum blossom on a long grass stalk, or fashion a daisy chain, or find out with a buttercup under our chins whether we liked butter.

They wore broad-brimmed sunhats that had seen many summers and were communal, kept with the deck chairs and rugs for sunny afternoons. They wore pearl necklaces and in the heat flung their cardigans around their shoulders, so that their bare arms in their sun frocks would not freckle. And in their ears were real gold earrings, which pulled slightly on the lobes so that you knew there must be a weight there.

'Do they hurt?'

And when they shook their heads to say no, you knew they could feel their earrings dance.

When we drew ladies on old envelopes and the backs of circulars we always gave them dancing earrings. Once my sister drew a lady with a wavy line across her front to be her bosoms, but someone said that was not nice, and not to do it again. So we gave our ladies handbags and earrings and frills and bracelets and umbrellas and high heels and hats and buttons and bows and no bosoms and that was all right.

But drawing was for winter, along with card playing and book reading. In summer it was out into the garden, into the standing gold of the afternoon sun where, dizzied with light and shade, we ran the dusty gravelled drive and found beyond bushes drumming with bumble bees, deep among bending grasses, the tank where frogs hopped.

The water was dark, sun-warmed, dusted with dropped seeds and skating insects. It was black, full of last year's crumbling leaves; impossible to tell how deep, or what lurked there. The little frogs when we caught them in the grass gleamed like jewels; their eyes were filigreed gold. We would set them in the water – 'Go, little frog' – and watch them spring downwards away from the sunlit surface to the deeper, secret layers of water.

We didn't tell about the frogs because the grown-ups would say, 'Go and wash your hands and don't touch frogs again.'

There was so much not to be touched, not to be looked at, not to be spoken of:

'Don't say that word.'

'Don't touch yourself there.'

'Don't go there. Grandpa's drowning kittens.'

And on summer days, 'Don't go near the beehives.'

From the aunts' rug we could see the row of white buzzing bee boxes sparkling in the distance through the rhododendrums and, moving among them, my grandfather in his black suit, his head in a black veil, his shoulders dusted with pollen, his hands full of honeycombs.

But someone always got stung. The bees always got us. Then shrieking with outrage we'd run for the aunts, because they could cure anything. They knew what to do about the bee sting still caught in the skin. They knew what to get from the kitchen to rub on the sore place. And if, overtired and overhot, the victim could not calm down they had the ultimate balm. One or other of them would take our sticky, grass-stained hands and lead us both into the house.

Once in the the living room she'd take the sufferer on her knee, and lift out the sewing box. It was proof against all woe. She'd slowly lift the lid with its waxed roses and we'd stroke the tightening red ribbons that held it angled open, but keep our fingers from the tempting padded satin underside, fat and glossy, frayed from the pins and needles that were stuck there.

'Don't touch, we don't want any more stings. Look – buttons.' She'd open a flat tobacco tin filled with pearl buttons of all sizes, right down to tiny ones, as small as the Os we practised in our writing books at school. They were for underwear of net and lace, light as a breath on the skin, and almost as transparent.

Then she'd take out the polished ebony box, long and thin, made to click shut so tightly you couldn't see the join. She'd pull gently and, greased and wrapped in paper, out would slide the steel needles used for knitting the finest of stockings, silk, before there were nylons. She'd pick one up and wipe away the grease. The steel would glint potent, sharp enough to pierce the heart – glamorous as the silken glinting ankle that made young men want to dance with you.

In the box, too, there were pink suspenders to replace the broken ones, and elastic for knickers that had long legs that you could tuck your hanky in, and this ravelledy knot? A garter, all stretching done.

'I kept it for the lace – a row of little hearts. Some day I will unpick it, and use it again.'

And a big coloured tangle of ends of embroidery threads.

'Fingers out. There could be needles. We were always embroidering: collars, blouses – and tray cloths and pillowcases for our bottom drawers. I did a beautiful nightdress of floppy pink, peachy stuff, soft as the softest skin. It went in my bottom drawer, and it's never been out. You can have it, whichever one of you gets married first.'

What else was in the sewing box? Thimbles, silver, worn; a darning mushroom to unscrew; old pennies, blackened; one jet button, one diamanté; hooks without eyes; rolled-up card glinting with press fasteners. We pored over all this paraphernalia, regalia of womanhood, tasted the hours spent over needlework – the frilling, flouncing, feathering forth … for the dance, the Sunday walk – the lowered eyes, the dropped, initialled handkerchief.

Not a one of my aunts ever married. In my memory they were not young women. In their handbags were lace-edged handkerchiefs, and tiny bottles of perfume. Sometimes they'd dab some on our wrists – and all day long we'd smell of violets.

Honeysuckle

IT WAS A WEDNESDAY – Maureen's visiting day, when she squeezed them in between work and home, where four children were waiting for their dinners. He told her about the honeysuckle in the backyard.

'What do you want with gardening at your age?' Maureen said.

'It'll give your dad something to look forward to,' she said.

'That honeysuckle will make your mother a nice view from the kitchen window,' he said.

'It'll make a nice scent in the summer,' she said.

They barely differentiated their thoughts, his from hers. They finished each other's sentences. At times they didn't need to speak, so well did each know the other's mind, grown old together, rolling along easily in their accustomed track.

'Tea,' he said, and went off into the kitchen.

She was knitting him a grey cardigan. Maureen frowned at the swollen knuckles awkwardly working the wool.

'That'll take you for ever. Better buy one.'

But she ignored the advice. Best way with our Maureen, she thought. Always spoiling for a fight. So she knitted on at the grey cardigan, slowly, very slowly, and the work was rough with poor tension, uneven and lumpy. But it was always there, something to work at, something to look forward to.

He brought in Maureen's tea, no sugar in that, and hers, left them on the little table, and shuffled back the few steps for his own mug and the packet of Rich Tea biscuits.

'You need new slippers,' Maureen said. 'You might slip. You might trip. Then what would you do?'

'Match on the telly,' he said.

'Well, how are things, any problems?' Maureen asked, as always.

Of course there never were. 'We're as you see us. And how are the children?'

And humbly they listened to all their doings.

'You must bring them round some day,' she said, as always.

'Good idea,' the daughter said, though it only ever happened at Christmas and birthdays.

'Well, I'm off,' Maureen said, leaving half her tea. 'No rest for the wicked. Anything you want doing before I go?'

And of course there never was.

And when she had gone, he said, as always, 'Very busy, our Maureen.'

'Hummpf,' she said.

Excepting Wednesdays, each day was the same. He would watch the TV, tend the fire, walk to the corner for their bits of shopping. She would knit, cook their sparse meals, rinse through nighties and socks. Maureen took the heavy washing to do in her machine at home. Good for Maureen, she'd thought when it was suggested, save my hands. For her hands were her one vanity. In the evening when her eyes were tired from her knitting, she'd rise and bring in from the scullery the Christmas or birthday bottle of hand lotion – always the same sort, his present to her.

And she'd join him on the sofa, in front of the TV, doing her hands, to a routine that never varied, making the bottle last by tipping out, carefully, carefully, a tiny pink pool of the lotion into the cup of her hand. Then she'd give the bottle to him and he'd lean forward and put it on the mantelpiece without moving his eyes from the TV. She'd sit still for a while, savouring the moment, warming the teaspoon of lotion in her palm to set free the scent of it, and then she'd bring her two palms together and rub, rub, rub.

Round and round, palms first, slick and oily, and then the fingers, slipping through each other, sliding smoothly, running joint through joint, her hands fluent again, stroking, smoothing, easing. They had a cleverness of their own. They knew by themselves how to pleat and smock the cloth for a baby's dress, how to make pastry, just right.

And so she'd been annoyed when he'd asked her to help make the bit of garden in the back yard. Her hands were for her own work. She didn't want to go grubbing in the earth, breaking fingernails, getting dirty. And then she remembered, long back, when they'd first bought the house, he'd been sorry there was no garden. 'Never mind,' he'd said. 'When I get up a bit we'll buy a bigger place, with a garden. You'll like a garden.'

She'd forgotten that he'd wanted her to have a garden.

She came round when he brought home the honeysuckle. He left it on the kitchen table until he got his breath back after the walk from downtown.

'I'll make you tea,' she said.

'Good plant that,' he said.

'Buy it?' she asked, annoyed at money wasted.

'Not much – reduced in a sale, but it's a good plant.' Then he had to struggle with his breathing again.

They drank tea, one on each side of the table, with the plant between them – an alien object clinging to its fragile bamboo prop, the questing tip of its stem reaching out blindly into the air.

'What is it then?' she asked. She knew nothing of plants, had no regard for them.

'Honeysuckle.'

'What's that then?'

'Climber. Goes up. It'll cover that wall. I'll put wire for it to climb on. And then next year, or the year after, when it's ready, it'll bloom. Lovely flowers, lovely scent.'

She looked again at the skinny, green plant on the

table. 'All that out of something so small?'

And then she drank her tea.

She helped him plant the honeysuckle.

'It'll be like a country lane out here, come summer. You'll see.'

She peeled the black plastic off the ball of roots. Moist compost fell into her hands. She cupped the roots in her hands. 'Is it hurt?' she asked.

'No.'

He shovelled away at a hole, putting in fertiliser, worked at the wall with wire and nails.

When he had finished she looked at the tiny sprig tied to the wire that stretched up the wall.

'And will it grow?' she asked.

'Oh aye. It knows how to grow,' he said.

That had been last summer, and now the honeysuckle had reached the top of its wire, and was a mass of green shoots and sprouts.

'It's done well,' he said. 'Pity it didn't bloom this year.'

'Never mind,' she said, taking his hand. 'I can wait.'

Witchwoman

DARLING NEVER KNEW WHAT DREW HER to the Witchwoman's house – drew her there even on the wintry days, when the trees were gaunt and the up-climbing road ran with cold rain.

'I can't keep that child at home,' her mother would say to the other women of the village. 'I don't know where she goes. She keeps secrets.'

'Oh, let her,' the others said. 'She is young and so sweet.'

They loved to take her in their laps and cosset her. There were so few children in their lives.

'She'll come to no harm. It's not like the old days.'

In the old days after their own men had gone to the war, strange soldiers roamed the woods, and after the fighting they stayed, only then they were starving and more dangerous. One who came too close to the village had been killed by the women. But that time had passed. The last of these men had left or died just around the time that Darling was born. No strangers came now. The women stitched and restitched their ragged clothes, waited for their own men to return, stirred pots of cabbage over smouldering fires and muttered one to the other, complaining. They formed a tight band. They would wait for the return of their own men and keep themselves safe. The old mothers among them kept their son's homes and wives in order.

The younger women loved Darling because of her brightness. They petted her and gave her what small treats they could devise: a doll plaited from wild straw, a handful of blackberries. They all knew, and nobody said or talked about it, that she was a child of rape, born from a vicious encounter when her mother in a mood of more than usual despair had wandered too far from the village. There was one other rape child in the village, an idiot boy, barely tolerated. He lolled in the mud. At night someone or other would throw a blanket over him. But Darling they adored, so fresh, so young, so blonde and blue-eyed. She was a reminder that life could be other than their present darkness, that deliverance would come.

They did not speak of the Witchwoman. There was much unspoken of in the village. Occasionally one of the old mothers would struggle up the hill for a cure. Darling had once followed one of these, concealing herself in the bracken as she went because it was her own grandmother, and this was the one woman in the whole village who would turn on her with a hard word and ungentle hand.

Darling was secretive by nature. When a child is too much watched over, she yearns for aloneness and Darling knew ways of disappearing in the woods, of vanishing even among the houses. This way she watched and learned the truth of many things. She learned that perhaps the men would never return, though the women kept their shirts aired and their tools sharpened. She learned too that her grand-mother hated her, but not why. Her childish under-standing could not piece together all the fragments of unguarded talk.

Darling had been told that the laneway went nowhere, and following it once had found it too broken and collapsed, too overgrown, to promise interest. She had turned back. There was something threatening in the grey-lichened trees that crowded around the laneway, their branches sweeping down almost to touch its surface, and shadowing it, dark as night. But if Grandmother could go that way, Darling would too, out of hatred and resentment of this one old woman who would not love her. If she could not have her affection, she would have her secrets. And so with all her wood skills she crept noiselessly through the twigs and leaves until she came out high along the laneway, and saw Grandmother disappear into a house that was almost invisible under a heavy growth of ivy. The length of Grandmother's stay outlasted Darling's curiosity and she slid her way back down through the wild woods to the village.

Her mother reproached her when she slipped through the doorway, home. 'Where have you been? You must tell me where you go.'

'Nowhere.' Darling knew her mother would not persist. Something in her mother always gave way to Darling. Instead of scolding she asked for a hug, and clung to her child in her accustomed, desperate way.

The old woman limped in, and Darling's mother

abruptly pushed the girl from her to hide the moment of affection. Grandmother was too preoccupied with her stick, the door latch and a bundle of leaves she carried to pay attention to her family. Darling's mother went to relieve her of the bundle, but the old woman snatched it closer, and snarled at her daughter-in-law.

'I would have fetched it for you, Mother,' the daughter-in-law said. 'It is a sore climb up there for you with your leg so bad.'

'I wanted to be sure I got what I asked for. You might have got notions on that long climb up and asked for something else. I know you.'

Darling's mother merely asked, 'Shall I get the poultice ready?'

'No,' said the old woman, and hobbled over to the hearth, setting down the bundle so carefully that Darling knew there was more to it than just leaves.

Her mother presently went to fetch water, and Darling followed her along the muddy street, taking hold of the handle of a pail as if her motive was to help.

'What has Grandmother brought?'

'Stuff to make a poultice for her leg.'

'Who gave it to her?'

Questions did not always bring answers, so she was glad when her mother said, 'The Witchwoman.

She lives on the hill above the village.' Her mother waved one empty bucket at the steep hill that frowned down upon the village. It was thick with trees, now just losing their autumn leaves, their mass adding to the oppressiveness of the height.

'Does she ever come down here? Did I ever see her?'

'No.'

'And she makes cures?'

'Not only cures, poisons too. She knows every leaf and twig, and the use of them.'

'Is she a bad woman?'

'People sometimes make bad use of her spells.'

'Here? In the village?'

'The mother of the idiot. Before he was born she went to the Witchwoman for something to kill him in the womb. It didn't work. It made him as he is – a punishment to her. And once, before the war, some cows were killed. No one knew by whom, but it was clear that it was witch work. Some of the men blamed the witch and wanted to kill her. But the women stopped them. They needed the cures. Some go for charms to keep their husbands safe, wherever they be.'

'Did you get one for Father?'

'No. I don't believe in such things. They are devil's work.' Her mother bent to dip the buckets under the surface of the pure clean well water. Darling hoped to hear more about the Witchwoman, but her mother was concentrating on getting the water home without spilling, and didn't speak.

When they got back to the house, they found that Grandmother had rolled herself up in a blanket and lay on the bed by the fire, her face to the wall. Leaves were crumbling in the ashes on the hearth. No one spoke as the buckets were set in place.

'It hurts,' Darling's mother whispered. 'The poultice burns away the badness in her leg.'

Silence was not unusual in that house. It brooded over the preparation of a thin porridge for supper. In the midst of the silence Darling, eating slowly at the table, thought her own thoughts, and knew that she'd go to the Witchwoman's house very soon, just to see.

For the next few days she stayed in the village, going from house to house, being petted and fed, helping with the work, hearing stories. The best storyteller was Marjory, a spinner, who was working on a rare fleece to spin wool for a blanket. She let Darling card and comb the rank-smelling wool and span stories and yarn together. Some of the wives would gather there – the lazy ones, the old mothers said – to listen as well. Darling's mother never came. The stories were wonderful, lilted out to the rhythm of the spinning wheel. There was laughter in this house, though it was here that the idiot boy lay under the table, twitching. Marjory had taken him in, fed him, washed him, called him her pet.

Darling would leave dazed by the tales, hardly seeing the mud and roughness of her own life, picturing instead the golden glories of kings and princesses. When she tried to repeat the tales to her mother she'd be hushed.

'It's nonsense. Life is hard enough without losing your head in dreams. Tend to the pig.'

So she thought her own thoughts, and kept a watch on the laneway, to see if anyone went that way. She felt reluctant to go alone to visit the Witchwoman, knowing somehow that it was an outrageous thing to do. But the prospect tugged at her. Only Marjory's tale-telling took it from her mind.

Then one day her grandmother gave her a beating, not an unusual occurrence, but this one hurt Darling in too many ways. She had thought herself alone in the house and was pretending to be a princess. She had made herself a crown with twigs and decorated it with ivy leaves. She wanted to admire herself. She knew that a mirror was kept in her grandmother's chest. It was a very precious thing and never used. She slid the chest from under the bed and, though this was forbidden, she opened it. There were folded lengths of cloth, a lock of baby's hair, a small black book with a cross on its cover, a bundle of ancient dried leaves, too frail to touch, and the mirror, a square of polished metal. But she didn't have a chance to pick it up.

Roaring beside her, purpled with anger, was Grandmother.

'How dare you, brat?'

'I only wanted the mirror.'

'The mirror! Vanity, evil, you child of evil!'

The old woman's words were choked out like writhing, biting demons. She dashed the twiggy crown from Darling's head and slapped her face with all her strength. Then, exhausted, she collapsed on the bed. Darling, broken and humiliated by her hurts, limped to the front door and escaped that narrow house.

The Witchwoman did not seem surprised to see her, nor was she as surprising a person as Darling had expected to find. She merely opened the door and stood studying Darling. The girl shuffled her feet, having no explanation for her presence.

'Come in,' the Witchwoman said, 'and I'll give you something for those bruises.'

The Witchwoman made her sit on a chair by the window, turned to the light. A row of plants stood on the windowsill. Beyond, through a gap in the trees, Darling could see over the top of another hill to more beyond, and further beyond that to where there was a great spread of smooth green land and beyond that mountains and beyond that the sky, vast and full of a golden light. It was almost sunset. The Witchwoman came to the window to take a nip of leaves from a plant and noticed Darling's spellbound gaze.

'You can see a long way from my house.' the Witchwoman said.

'So much beyond.'

'Did you come from the village?'

'Yes,' Darling said. 'In the village there is no beyond, and the sky is small. The hills and the trees hide it.'

'That is why I like to live up here. You can see the bigness of things.' The Witchwoman went back to a pot on the stove that she stirred slowly, dropping in the leaves and murmuring under her breath.

'I can't see the village,' Darling said.

'It is below us, out of sight.' The Witchwoman was very tall, not old or young. Her face was smooth but her hands were workworn, and she wore her hair under an old woman's bonnet. There was a deep silence in the house, a wrapped-away, undisturbed ancient silence, not like the silence of Darling's home, which was barbed and bitter, full of averted faces and turned backs. This was a silence that was like a deep in-drawn breath that was just as gently expelled, huge slow breaths that went on and on as if the sky was breathing. There was a cat watching mute by the hearth, the murmur of a kettle nearly boiling, the smallest drawing of the Witchwoman's spoon across the bottom of the pot as she stirred. Darling felt she could hear dust fall.

The Witchwoman set the pot to cool on the table, and laid a clean folded cloth beside it. She came and sat by Darling, folding her hands in her lap, sitting very straight. Her eyes were on a level with Darling's. Darling had lost her sulkiness and offence at Grandmother's attack. She had lost her panic and outrage. She merely sat, waiting for what the Witchwoman would tell her.

'You are called Darling, aren't you?'

Darling nodded.

'That is not your real name. It is not the name your mother gave you. It is a pet name made up by the village women.'

'I didn't know.'

'Your mother called you Freedom. No one could understand the giving of such a name. It was never used. But I will call you that. Real names are important. My real name is Dame Johanna. You will call me that. I know what they call me in the village and it is not true. I am not a wicked woman. I won't allow you to come here if you are going to be frightened of me.'

Darling nodded.

'I think the lotion is ready. It will ease the pain and take away the bruising.'

Then Dame Johanna fetched the cloth, dipped it in the pot and washed Darling's face and shoulders. The warmth of the lotion stayed in her skin, easing the soreness.

'Now you must go. It will be dark soon. Your mother will be worried. She is a good woman. Tell no one you were here, or they will set a watch to stop you coming again.'

And so it began, Darling's apprenticeship, though she did not know it to be such. She was taking her first steps in a deep learning, on a dangerous path. She knew only that the peace and ease in her life came to her in the Witchwoman's house, where she was told the names of plants and how and when to gather them, what cutting implement to use, how to preserve those that needed it, and what their properties were. She avoided her grandmother and resented the tittle-tattle of the village women who stroked her hair, but hadn't called her by her real name. She was gentle with her mother because now she could see her suffering at the old woman's hands.

Then uproar came to the village. One of the men returned. The women flew into a sort of panic. They did not seem to know what to do. They clustered around him, naming their husbands, their sons; where were they? had he seen them? when would they come? He had huddled by the fireside, un-responsive under his cloak of sacking, unable or unwilling to speak, until his wife and mother drove the others from the house.

Some of the women began to keep a vigil at the head of the road to the village. If one man came home, why not another, or all of them? Agitation ran through the village. Tempers flared. The idiot boy's mother came to fetch him from Marjory's house. There was a screaming battle – Marjory did not want to give him up. All the women and old mothers gathered at the door with a terrible insistence that he should be given back. Marjory had to let them take him. She called Darling to her and whispered, 'Help this boy. Follow the women, find where they leave him and then take him to the Witchwoman. And don't return. You must never come back. The witch might change you to a frog, but these women will kill you.'

'My mother . . .'

'She can't stop them now. The old woman wants it. Now go, run, hide.'

Darling followed the women. In a clear space, puddled with water, lashed by the wind, the mother laid down the boy, unrolled the blanket he was wrapped in and undressed him, piling his clothes onto the blanket. He whimpered, naked and pale on the ground. She watched him a moment, then rolled up the bundle of clothes, stowed it to keep dry under her shawl. 'Go to sleep,' she said to the boy, and without another glance turned quickly back down the hill to the village.

The boy lay still now, his spidery limbs folded up around him. Darling waited for the women to get well away, but just as she was about to leave her hiding place she heard another, louder tramp of feet and men came through into the clearing. To Darling they seemed to speak with the voices of dogs, barking out their words. They clanked with swords and staves and baggage. One of them poked the boy with his booted foot, and then made as if to kick his head.

'Leave it. It's half-dead.'

'Witch's spawn.'

'Devil's spawn. She's had her way too long, while we've been away.'

'Aye, but we'll get her now. We'll hunt her out, and all her doings.'

And then they left, tramping on towards the village, their noise echoing off the enclosing hills.

Darling approached the boy. His eyes were brown and frightened like an animal's. He must have been about her age, but she could carry him easily. Dame Johanna set both of them by the fire to warm. She wrapped the boy in a soft woollen blanket. His jerking grew less. Some peacefulness came into his eyes.

'There are men in the woods.'

'I know,' Johanna said. 'We will have to go, if we are to have our freedom, and our lives.'

'Where?'

'Beyond. There is always beyond.'

The tree

THE SKY SAGGED OVER THE BACK YARD like a big wet grey tent, while the drip drip drip of the weary rain was marked in the puddle around the bin by endless little circles, coming going, coming going, coming going. It was not good rain to watch. It was the very worst sort of rain. Mary Ann, watching through the window by the kitchen sink, scolded herself. That sort of rain could only bring dark thoughts, and long ago, oh many years ago, when the lonely years began, she had made a promise to herself to turn away from the dark thoughts. If, in her solitude, she had any duties left to her, the one clear one was to keep herself cheerful.

Anyway, the rain was set for the day. It would not stop now and it was getting dark. But it wouldn't keep her from her errand. She gathered up the lunchtime cup and plate she'd been washing and put them in the dresser. Then, going carefully down on her hands and knees, she slid an old cardboard box out of the cupboard below. She brought it to the table and set it down there with the greatest of care. For this was a ceremony. Today was the day she would buy her Christmas tree.

Not one Christmas had gone past, and she'd seen many go – but she'd had her tree. And fine trees they had all been, perfectly symmetrical and heavily scented, all shining with the lights on them, sparkling and shivering with tinsel. A Christmas tree was a magic thing. Yes, she said to herself, that was the word – magic. They were like ladies, all those trees, all done up in their finery, fit to go waltzing under chandeliers. And I have all their ornaments, all kept safe. She stroked the box as if it held a miser's treasure.

But enough dreaming. She tied her plastic rainhood

under her chin with a brisk knot, and scurried out quickly past the ancient tree in her tiny garden, for its bare branches always gathered up extra fistfuls of rain to fling down as if in spite.

She warmed her heart, as she trotted along, with memories of other Christmas expeditions made years ago when she'd been a wee lass, dodging along through the rain in her mother's wake. It had always been this time of day, when the light was beginning to go. Out they'd set to buy a scarf for a present for Daddy, oranges for stockings for the wee ones, maybe a silver star for the tree. And she'd never minded the rain then, not a bit of it – for in the half-light it had decorated the town with coloured reflections of shop windows and streetlamps. It had splashed and puddled brightly underfoot, and fell in gleaming splinters of haphazard light. And she'd never minded, either, the gathering darkness – for it fore-shadowed the magic darkness of long-awaited Christmas Eve, when the very blackness of night vibrated with expectation.

The same childish exaltation came back to her now as she bobbed through the wet Christmas crowds, and here before she expected it was the shop where Christmas trees lay in a soaking pile under the falling rain.

*

'Ach, 'tis yourself, then,' the man was saying. 'Come to choose your tree then?'

'I have.'

'Want it delivered, same as last year?'

'That would be very good of you. Next door has a key and can let it in if I'm not home first.'

'I doubt if you will be. The van will be away in ten minutes.'

'I'd better choose quickly then.'

But she chose also with due care among the green trees, for to her they were all people, all wishing, like Cinderella, to go to the ball, to escape the lamplit needles of rain. Never mind, you shall all go to the ball, whispered Mary Ann, the fairy godmother. She hoped, as she paid for her special tree, that her foolish thoughts were well hidden from the sensible shop man.

'My dear,' a loud voice hailed her. 'Whatever are you doing out in weather such as this? You must take care of yourself, at your age.'

Mary Ann's heart sank. This woman was one of those bullying people who would not allow the meek of the world to go on their own timid way, but perpetually interfered, knowing best. She awoke a consistent dread in Mary Ann.

'But I had to come out,' Mary Ann said, her face twitching with embarrassment. 'I had to get my tree.'

'A Christmas tree – at your age, my dear?' the woman asked. 'Now if you'd take my advice you'd spare yourself the trouble. They make a terrible mess of the house, and it's all a con by the shopkeepers anyway – making a fortune out of selling bushes – not to mention all those rubbishy decorations. I don't know how people can be taken in so easily – wasting good money on stuff that's only fit to be thrown away the day after Christmas – total nonsense –'

'But a Christmas tree is so pretty,' Mary Ann faltered.

'Pretty!' the woman guffawed. 'My goodness, what does pretty have to do with anything at our time of life? Far better save your pension for something sensible – invest in a few thermals – but I mustn't keep you – happy Christmas.'

And away the woman went, steering a central course along the pavement, the stream of people parting on either side of her.

Her words had fallen on Mary Ann like the chillest of rain, had drenched all her bright little fires of memory. She clenched her bony hands in their woollen gloves and was surprised to feel hard coins against her palm. Change from the Christmas tree. She had forgotten all about it. Well, she'd show that stupid woman what she thought of her – she'd go right now and buy a new ornament for her tree. New things were very rare and very exciting in Mary Ann's life, and something new, some shiny, wonderful gift, was just what she needed to prove that her tree was a beautiful and a necessary thing.

She turned abruptly into the first shop door she came to – it was a big shop and she was not used to such places. The confusion and noise of the place seemed to enter into her brain. At last she found the Christmas decorations, but her expectations left her as she gazed along the tousled counter. There were heaps of tangled tinsel, coloured glass balls tumbled this way and that, some of them broken – and layers of ticketed plastic ornaments. She picked up a plastic Santa Claus, but his printed face was crooked and he remained just what he and all the other things were – unmagic, meaningless, made by the thousand – cheap and heartless, meant to be thrown away the day after Christmas. No, these things would not do – there was nothing here that could restore her Christmas tree. Still, she bought a string of tinsel because she could never leave a shop empty-handed, and because she was still pretending that all was well within her. She paid and put the tinsel into her shopping bag without pride and went back out into the rain.

Perhaps it was just a foolishness – an old woman's

silliness – to pretend that something pretty could be made at the dark time of the year. Life was like a bare tree, open to the rain – what could you possibly find to hang on its branches that was gorgeous enough to warm the heart? Perhaps it's as well to see things in this light, she thought. I suppose it's more real, and real things are better than pretend, or so they tell us.

It took her a long time to get home, for her small frame seemed heavy to her, and the rain had found its way through the thin stuff of her coat, and was leaning with cold hands on her shoulders. When she reached the doorstep she paused to regard the blackened, dripping tree in the garden. That's me, she thought, nothing will brighten my branches again. She gave herself a little shake of annoyance. There, she thought, I've gone and let that rain get at me, and she put her key in the lock without expectation.

Her next-door neighbour stood in the hallway. He was saying something. It took a while for her to understand.

'The children have made a surprise for you . . . they came in with me when I let the tree in. I do hope you won't mind. You see, they found the box of decorations. Come and see.'

And there in the darkened room stood a glowing Christmas tree, perfectly symmetrical, scented, gleaming like a candle flame. And here were the children, bouncing with excitement.

'We put the decorations on, for a surprise – and there's new decorations on too – we made them for you in school – can you see them?'

But Mary Ann could not see them, for the tree was a glorious, golden blur, where all the little trinkets seemed to shift and shimmer until they looked not like themselves at all.

'I made this robin,' one child cried, bringing a cardboard bird of uneven wingspan.

'And I made this bell,' the other said, 'but it's not a real bell. It doesn't ring. But we can always pretend.' And she jiggled the bell on its branch, to fill the room with the pretend music of its pretend ringing.

'I do hope you don't mind,' the man was saying.

'Ah no, no, it's a beautiful surprise, the best surprise...' Mary Ann's mousy voice hid all her feelings. 'I don't mind at all. It's a lovely tree. And I've brought something new for it too.'

She added her length of shop tinsel to the spiky branches, and was able to say, 'There now, it doesn't look too bad at all, does it?'

Pilgrim

S HE ARGUED WITH TOM when he was back late from the fishing trip. 'You knew I wanted the car. You're late on purpose, to stop me going,' she said.

'That's not true.'

'You hate me going, you always have.'

'I just think it's a bad idea. Look at you, you're

already upset and you're not even there yet. Let me go with you.'

'You're no part of it. Let me alone.' She snatched the keys from his hand and rushed off to the car.

It was late when she reached the beach. It would soon be dark. She wouldn't have much time. She had wanted to be alone, unhurried, careful. Now it was spoiled. She got out and slammed the car door, only then realising that she had forgotten the flowers – a handful of wind-bruised garden flowers. 'Oh damn.' She kicked at the sand that had drifted over the car park. 'It's spoiled. There's no point now.' But she didn't want to go back in a temper. Might as well walk it off. Face the beach, no matter what her frame of mind. She drove her hands deep into the pockets of her padded coat and sank her chin into its collar. A sharp wind blew from the sea. She bowed her head against it, the first breath of autumn, and set off along the broken concrete path that led to the shore. She passed a weatherworn sign that said, 'BATHING IS DANGEROUS BEYOND THE GREEN MARKERS.'

That was new. There were more visitors now, she supposed, more strangers who didn't know the tricks of the tide.

She came out onto the beach. It had always been an unfriendly shore, the waves man-high and driven so fiercely landwards that they gouged deep channels among ever-shifting sand bars. A steep hill to her right climbed so abruptly that it seemed to hang its grey and green bulk over the sea, menacing the water. To her left the beach stretched for an even mile, broken by a long spit of stones that reached far out into the bay, dividing and confusing the water so that the waves ran crosswise, confounding each other.

And then she froze, for two boys dashed past her from the dunes by the car park. They wore only gaudy shorts and shrieked at the chill of the wind. Yet they pelted down the shore and urged each other into the water. She had to watch. They leaped and howled through the first breakings of the water, were suddenly wading thigh deep, and then again as suddenly were racing over the sand bar, before descending abruptly chest-deep among the waves. They had gone far out and were tiny figures among the dashing waves before she could turn aside. She would not watch them. She must not watch them. She turned sideways to the wind, relieved to escape its eye-watering strength, and walked quickly along the sand, partly to keep warm and partly to get away from the bathers.

Tomorrow she and Tom must go home. Here used to be home. She had so much wanted Tom to see this western coast, where she'd grown up. She'd told him about this beach, about what had happened here, how she must make her pilgrimage, and he'd understood at first. They'd had a good time so far. They really had. He'd enjoyed meeting her family, being teased and spoiled – our Susan's sweetheart. It set a seal on their togetherness.

'How could you leave such a lovely place?' he'd asked, and her face had darkened.

'Are you still going to go . . . there?' he'd asked.

'Yes.'

'When?'

'When I'm ready.'

Perhaps you're never ready for a thing like this. She had wanted to approach this shriving with composure. Instead she was cross, having shrieked at Tom like a fishwife, slapped away his restraining hand, forgotten the flowers. It was not tears in her eyes, it was the wind. She especially regretted the flowers, they were to have been a peace offering to the past, because the time had come when the future at last seemed bright again. There was no grave to bring flowers to. The sea had not even been generous enough to return him.

She had fled this place, gone as far away from here as she could, yet images had pursued her, persecuted her – of dashing waves, screaming seagulls, sand gritty below her feet, and far out in the water a dark head rising on the waves, falling and rising among the crests and finally, in that last, heart-stopping aeon of moments, not rising. That was what had haunted her – the empty waves. And though she had absented herself, drawn a curtain of strange places, new people between herself and that day, she had thought at one time that she would never be free of that moment. Then Tom had come along and she had taken a hold on life again.

Without realising, she had already come to where the spit of stones ran out into the water. The stones were grey, round and hard as fists. She walked along the top of the bank, away from the reaching surf, and looked out over the water, just as she had watched that day.

He had been young and giddy, full of daring. That had made him swim that day. So many years ago. She tried now to recall him, how he had looked, spoken, moved, what they had talked about on all those long youthful evenings. It was all gone. All washed away. She had said, 'Don't swim today. It's too rough.' But heedless as a fish he stripped and ran into the water, turning with one last laugh to mock her timidity. She tried so hard to picture him, the dark head turned back towards her, laughing defiantly. That was how he was made, filled to the brim with careless, ranging energy. That was why he had chosen the water, plunging into waves that swept him away as though he had never been. If he had lived would he ever have settled down? Like Tom? She could see Tom clearly, the brown eyes hurt and sullen over how she had attacked him. And she knew at that moment that she loved Tom too well to want to hurt him. She need never doubt her love for him.

That first boy had marked her life, but first love is a thing apart. Who knew what would have happened had he been a different person, content to dally with her on the shore? He had made his choice and years later she had made hers.

She felt a deep calmness. The waves as she watched became mere waves, not threatening beasts. She turned to go, but then paused, still wanting to make some last gesture, do something to mark her forgiveness. But what? She stood empty-handed.

And then, like a ghost, the dark-headed boy came back to her, gazing into her eyes, tender and tentative because he had just given her her first kiss. And then he had broken away, down to the waterline, eyes on the ground as if abashed. He had returned with the whitest, smoothest stone he could find, egg-shaped and of a size to fit the palm of her folded hand.

'So that you don't forget today,' he had said. And she had not forgotten. Now it was tears, not the wind, in her eyes, and they were warm. The sea had not washed him entirely away. That part of herself was returned to her. She knew now what to give him and searched for a white stone, egg-shaped to fit her palm. And threw it as hard as she could. It did not fly far into the gobbling surf. She could not see where it fell. But she was ready to go home now to Tom, to seek him out and put her arms around him and let him know that all was completely mended.

Bridie Birdie

I WASN'T TO SPEAK TO BRIDIE BIRDIE any more than I needed to, Mother said, Bridie was a bad influence, Bridie had a dark soul. Don't make a friend of her. It would do you no good.

Bridie Birdie lived alone in the little house at the end of the back lane. It was a tiny house, white with a pointy roof, and a little garden of cabbages and spuds beside it. Bridie had her own door through the old high wall, to let her out onto the old road. She kept it always locked and bolted. You wouldn't know from the road that the little house was there, except for the smoke from the chimney.

Sometimes when Daddy took me for a walk and we were caught by the rain on the way back, we'd make a run for Bridie Birdie's gateway in the wall. He'd bang on it and holler. I'd stand all hunch-shouldered in the rain, waiting for the sound of the bolt being pulled back. Bridie Birdie was always slow to open her door, but we'd forgive her at the thought of the shelter we'd get, once inside her little house. And I loved her house.

There were pines let grow tall all around it, so that even before you got into the house, you were already out of the rain and the wind – standing on a carpet of old pine needles while Bridie Birdie fumbled the bolt back into its catch. She locked everything. In her mind burglars were sneaking through every open door, and climbing over walls no matter how high. She had had Daddy set broken glass in a layer of cement all along the top of the high wall beside her house and garden. She must surely have felt safe enough.

'You'll catch your death from the rain,' she'd say and shush us on into the house and then lock and bolt us all safely inside. It was very dark inside because of the trees around. If there was much wind the trees would sing down the chimney and blow smoke down, so that your eyes watered and you coughed.

We weren't often in Bridie Birdie's house, but because of the warning about her dark soul I was especially attentive. I thought that the dark soul had to do with the dark house and tried to learn all I could of it. I tried to puzzle out the shadowy corners, the contents of the high shelves. I would sit on a wooden stool up against the hearth where my coat would dry out, while Bridie Birdie and Daddy talked.

Bridie Birdie would set the black kettle over the fire to boil and put out thick white cups and saucers on the table under the window. There was no cloth on the table, only the bare white boards. On the other side of the hearth from where I sat, on a cushion on the hob, was a black cat, round as the kettle, its paws tucked under its chest and its head up watching us. I would try to outgaze its yellow eyes, but I never succeeded. That cat could outstare the devil.

Once on our way home I asked Daddy why Bridie Birdie was called Birdie.

'It's her name. She was married to a sailor from over the water. He didn't stay long and left her with one child. The child died of tuberculosis. Bridie had a long spell in hospital herself. She's had a hard life.'

'Is that why she has a dark soul, because of the hard life?'

'That's bad talk. Where did you get that from? There's nothing dark about Bridie Birdie. She's as playful as a child, and as innocent.'

But when we got home it was 'I suppose you've been in with Bridie Birdie again. I told you not to take Sally there.'

'It was pelting down, and there's no harm in the old woman.'

Nothing more was said, but my coat was whisked off me so sharply I knew there was harm somewhere.

Bridie's groceries came home along with ours because she couldn't make it to the shops on her own. The cardboard boxes of goods would be left on the kitchen table to be sorted by mother and Mrs Deans. Our stuff would go in the cupboards and larder, and Bridie's into the smallest of the cardboard boxes, and one of the boys would take it up the back lane. Sometimes Daddy would slip in an extra packet or two and Mother would scold. 'What are you doing? She'll only think the worse of you for that.'

'Och, sure it's nothing.' And then he'd leave the room. He couldn't put up with being scolded. The extra packets would stay in the box.

Sometimes when I knew for sure that no one saw me I'd put in a little present of my own – maybe some daisies tied with a thread, or a rose from the garden. Once I put in my red hair ribbon, and another time a brooch with stones missing out of it. Nobody wanted it. I had found it in the button box.

It was very quiet for me at home. The boys were too big to be bothered with me. Anyway, they were boys, going about shouting and kicking off heavy boots that thundered over the floor. So I was on my own most of the time which is why I so very much liked watching and noticing. I was very good at it.

I noticed Mother and Mrs Deans weren't speaking long before Mrs Deans left because of her sciatica. That happened around the same time that her Agnes stopped walking by up the mountainy road. Sometimes our Donnie would go with her. I saw him hide his bike behind the high wall, and climb over it, when he was supposed to be going into town. And I knew that Agnes Deans must have been waiting for him on the other side. I could hear their voices. And once I saw them far away in one of the top fields, dancing and dancing until they fell down together in the long rushy grass. It must have been damp.

When Mrs Deans left, Agnes never walked up the mountain road again, and Donnie went to Scotland, to friends of Daddy's, to learn their ways of working the land. 'Until he settles himself,' Mother said.

On the next Saturday, Mother showed the new girl how to sort the groceries, then went upstairs to lie down. Jack began to yell at Daddy. He said there was too much to do about the place now that Donnie was away, and wasn't it well for Donnie to be out of it. Daddy said he wouldn't be talked to like that, and Jack went out banging the door behind him. So there was nobody to take Bridie Birdie's box over, only Daddy. He looked at his watch and said he had business that couldn't be left, and the goods couldn't wait about or they'd spoil, I'd have to take the box over. He lifted it onto the carrier of Donnie's bike, and though it was too big for me to ride, I could push it – and it was only a short way up the lane.

I was breathless with excitement as I knocked on Bridie Birdie's door. Would she be wearing the red hair ribbon, or the brooch?

'Och, is it you?' she said once she got the door opened. 'Come in, rest yourself.'

As I took my seat by the fire, she lifted the box onto the table, and fastened the three locks on the back of her door.

'Do you keep the door always locked up?'

'Oh yes, you never know what's out there.'

'Sure, there'd be nothing out there. There's never burglars around here, and they'd only go for the well-off sort of people.'

'Well I wasn't talking only about burglars.'

'About what then?''

'Things, just. Now will you take a ginger nut for your trouble?'

I said that I would, and waited for her to find the packet in her box. She was methodical and did not rush. The black cat stared from its cushion on the hob.

'Oh dear,' said Bridie Birdie from the table. 'There's no present from the fairies today. They usually put me in a little something – some wee sort of a thing.'

'What wee sort of a thing?'

'All sorts of wee things. I have them in my tin box. That's where I keep my secret things and I'm not about to show them to the likes of you till I know if you can keep secrets.'

'I know lots of secrets.'

'And you wouldn't be about to tell me any, just to prove it, would you?'

'That would be daft.'

'Well, you've a head on your shoulders at least. We'll see about the secrets as we go on. Will you be back?'

'I don't know.'

Then she gave me a ginger nut and began snapping back the bolts on the door to let me out.

*

Mother never noticed that I was taking the box to Bridie's. She spent more time resting and would leave the sorting to me and the new girl. The new girl was called Betty and wasn't as good as Mrs Deans. Mother didn't like her being so young, and what about Jack in and out of the kitchen? She wanted no more disasters. But Jack caused no disasters in the kitchen. He was out over the fields every day, or in town with Daddy, learning the ropes.

Sometimes he stayed on late in town, and one morning Betty found his bed hadn't even been slept in. Mother said, 'Give that boy enough rope and he'll hang himself.' One night coming home drunk he fell roaring down the stairs and woke us all up. Mother said he needed the knotted end of a rope across his back, that was how her father had ruled his sons, but it was obvious there was to be no discipline in this house. There was bad blood in this family with all their go-to-the-devil ways and it wasn't from her they had it and she rued the day she'd crossed the threshold of this house.

Daddy didn't say anything. He got Jack up the stairs and into his room, and then he put me to bed. He tucked me up tight and kissed my forehead, but he looked sad and quiet. He didn't put Mother to bed, because I could hear her slippers going up and down the landing, up and down. And then I went to sleep.

I had a skipping rope with knots on the ends. I knew Daddy wouldn't hit Jack with it, but I hid it the next morning. And because I was angry with Mother I took the lilac gloves she wore on Sundays from the drawer in the hall table.

Bridie Birdie was delighted with them when she found them in her grocery box. 'Would you look at that? Aren't the fairies good to me? Look at the little shape of them.' She laid one of the gloves over the back of her big red hand. The glove looked tiny and reached only halfway down her fingers.

'Sure they'd do you better nor me.'

'I've got gloves,' I said.

'I'll put them in the tin box with all me other things. Aren't they soft and light, and look at the colour of them. Sure I only ever saw flowers that colour.'

'Maybe they're the sort of gloves fairies wear,' I lied.

'Maybe so, to go dancing.'

'Do they dance in our fields?'

'Do they not? They were dancing in your fields before they were your fields. Why do you think I keep the doors locked tight. This is a terrible mischievous area for fairies – it's too close to the mountains.'

'Did you see them dancing ever?'

'No I did not. I'd not be going out in the dark looking for dancing fairies. But I'll tell you where you'd find some.'

'Where?'

'In the field over beyond the beech avenue.'

'Right by the house?'

'The one with the big grey stones in. But here I am, nearly telling you a secret. Away sharp with you.'

And I found myself outside with my ginger biscuit, listening to the bolts of her door shooting home, snap, snap, snap.

I said to Betty about fairies dancing in our fields.

'Where'd you get that from?'

'Bridie Birdie.'

'Sure that's only an oul yarn she's spinning you. That one's away with the fairies herself.'

But that night I did get out of my tightly tucked-in bed to shiver my way over the lino and peep out at the moonlit night. I could see that field from my bedroom, and there was the row of man-sized stones crossing the field. But that's all there was. In the bright moonlight I could see that clearly.

Mother's headaches got worse. She said she had to sleep in a room by herself because of them. Some days she didn't get out of bed at all and Betty had to bring

her meals upstairs on trays. When Mother ate upstairs
the rest of us ate in the kitchen along with Betty. We
didn't bother with the dining room which was always
cold, even with a fire lit. I liked eating at the bare
kitchen table. It was warm and the dishes made a
pleasing thump on the bare wood. Betty never fussed
if stuff got spilled, and Jack could tilt his chair back as
far as he liked.

Jack said that the dining room was full of ghosts: all
the Evanses that had ever eaten there, sitting on each
other's laps down all the generations. He said that in
his usual dining-room chair he could feel the bones of
at least five knobby old ancestors under him. Daddy
slapped the boards of the table, and roared laughing.
Betty laughed too, but I knew, in the way that I knew
all sorts of things, that Betty half believed Jack and
was glad to be out of the dining room. Jack was
getting out of his bad moods. That was nice.

The next thing the fairies gave Bridie Birdie was a
grey chiffon scarf. It looked like something a fairy
would wear, and Bridie Birdie was enchanted by it.
Under the yellow gaze of the black cat she held it up
by the two corners. 'Would you look at that! Sure
what are they thinking of sending me a thing like
that. It's as thin as a shadow! There'd be no heat in

that! But isn't it just the bee's knees of a gorgeous thing! Looka me!'

She threw it over her head like a veil and hushed. I could see the glint of her eyes behind the transparent grey. I shifted my gaze to the yellow-eyed black cat, because Bridie Birdie in her grey veil was too much of a ghost.

'Hah! Scared you.' She laughed, snatching the scarf from her head.

'I looked in that field,' I said. 'You were wrong. There's no fairies in it.'

'Indeed and there are. Man-big and looking at you. What do you think the stones are?'

'Stones.'

'They're stones now, but they didn't always used to be stones. First they were fairies, dancing fairies.'

'How did they get to be stones?'

'The fairy women danced in the field by moonlight. They were more beautiful than anything you could imagine. There was fairy music too, and when the men heard the music they came to watch the dancing and the women found out and they were jealous as sin. So they ran for blankets and threw them over the dancing fairies to hide the sight of them. And the blankets turned to stone. You go and look at those stones and if the sun's in the right place you'd maybe see a face in the stone, but as if behind a veil, or a knee or a hand, jutting up into the surface of the stone.'

'That's horrible. That's too sad.'

The cat rose, yawned a pink yawn and settled again, blinking its yellow eyes at me. It didn't care about the fairies in the stones.

That night I had terrible dreams and woke screaming, fighting against the tucked-in blankets that held me down in the bed. I woke everyone. For a while I didn't know they were there. I didn't even see the light when they switched it on.

'It's dark. It's dark,' I kept calling. 'The cloth has darkened me.'

'What is this all about?' I heard my mother's voice at last. 'Speak to me. I'm here.' She was holding me tight, very tight. She smelt clean and safe.

'Out there in the hay field. The fairies are in the stones. I can hear them screaming.'

'It's just a dream.'

'It's not, Bridie Birdie told me.'

'It's stupid stories. It's only stones. You'll see by daylight.'

In the morning Daddy said that I was never to go to see Bridie Birdie again. It wasn't allowed. Mother didn't go for her rest that afternoon. 'Headache or no headache, it's clear someone needs to take charge around here.'

Betty was sent to spread the cloth on the dining-room table. We were going to eat there, and we did, with freshly ironed napkins covering our laps.

I had the dream again that night and for many nights. Coping with it seemed to give Mother strength. 'It only proves me right,' she snapped at Daddy. 'I should have kept a better eye on things.'

There were no more headaches. She decided I needed dancing lessons, to civilise me and give me the chance to mix with my own sort. We stood in rows, counting the steps. One two three hop, one two three hop. The dreams stopped after a while. Dullness settled upon me like a blanket of snow. I forgot.

One day a black cat came to the kitchen windowsill. It stared at us with yellow eyes. Betty tried to frighten it away with a flapping tea towel, but it wouldn't go. When Daddy came in from his work and saw it there he said, 'I know that cat,' and he went out again. He was away a long time. When he came back he was weary. He said he had had a hard time breaking in, what with all the bolts. That there was nothing he could do for her, only pull the blanket up over her face. Bridie Birdie had died, bird-alone.

'Well,' mother said. 'Well . . .'

Ghosts

YOU HAVE WAITED NEAR THE PORCH DOOR for an hour, patient as a cat waiting to be let in. And now Aunt bustles up, rings the doorbell, knocks, flings the door open and strides in shouting, 'Harry, Harry, where are you?'

You follow noiselessly and disappear among the shadows of the hallway, taking secret repossession of the house, by stealth, not by right. Aunt's voice comes from upstairs where she is bullying Harry out of bed. 'Crying into your pillow won't bring her back ...'

Quickly, while no one is about, you cross the hall and tip your head down here by the keyhole, where the keyhole cover is stuck up sideways with thick cream paint, forever accommodating the eavesdropper. Not that you need a keyhole to hear the shrieks and giggles of two overexcited little girls romping over the sofa and trampling a favourite uncle. But you must hide again. Here come the commanding footsteps. Aunt intrudes.

'Stop that at once, girls. That's no way to behave. You do not jump on the chairs.'

'Oh let them, just this once,' says the uncle.

'What are you thinking of? It's hardly fitting, their poor mother not yet ...' But she stops short.

There has been a great fluster in the house – a great busyness. This thin aunt has a hold of the house like a rug and is shaking it, shaking it. She has visited every corner with her duster and broom and you, turned out of all your hiding places, have flitted before her from one room to the next. It's almost as if she knew you were here and sought to banish you. But it would take sharper senses than Aunt's to perceive you. She does not see the tiny whorl of dust where you pass, the shivering of the curtain that you stand beside.

But now it's dark, and the house is inhabited by broad, hospitable shadows. Here you are safe and can watch the hallway, where Aunt marches to and fro, marshalling visitors into the front room. There comes the gentle clicking of the girls' shoes on the shiny red lino of the deserted hall. They've been overlooked and do not want to join the long-faced adults. Here in the lamplit hall life is as it used to be. They start an old game. They pretend that the polished lino is ice. They take off their shoes and slide up and down the hall in their stockinged feet. They start quietly, but get more and more excited. They experiment with sliding backwards, and then the bigger girl crashes, with a yelp, into the hall table. A potted fern topples. Instinctively you start out of your sheltering shadow to help, but there is nothing you can do, not now. Besides, Aunt is there. They make their accustomed excuse: 'We were shining the floor.'

'I'll shiny you. You two are nothing but trouble, all day. You are bad, bad girls. Get up to bed. At once.'

The girls stand their ground for a moment: 'Can we have our biscuits?'

'What biscuits?'

'We always get biscuits.'

'You'll get no biscuits tonight. Now no buts . . .'

Up in their unlit bedroom, where the big brown wardrobe that so terrifies the smaller girl is all swollen up in the darkness, there is muted crying – and it is not for biscuits.

Below in the kitchen there is a murmured conversation.

'You are such a support to Harry. What would he do without you?'

'Oh I don't know if I help. I get so cross with the girls – I'm just not used to children. They make such a noise. I'm exhausted, and Harry won't do anything, he won't take notice of anybody or of anything you say, just sits there. It's dreadful, the whole thing.'

'Tragic,' the friend says. 'I think we'll need both teapots, don't you? Such a crowd.'

'And Harry, just sitting there, looking at the floor . . .'

The girls are having a bath: you can hear their happy commotion all over the house. It draws you in through the open bathroom door. It's safe enough, you won't be seen; the plastic curtain is half drawn alongside the bath to minimise splashes. The pink limbs of the children are dimly visible through it. Steam cloaks everything. Moisture runs on the walls. The bath brims with soapy water. The girls brim with delight. Their laughter slops over the edge of the bath and threatens to flood the house. You are laughing too, but your voice is faded to an infinite softness.

Thin, pained authority intervenes from below with a mighty shout. 'Girls! I won't tell you again. You must be quiet and not upset your father.'

A sudden shriek escapes the bathroom.

Aunt, again exasperated, calls from the foot of the stairs. 'Now what is it?'

'I've soap in my eye.'

'Don't make such a fuss then. You would worry a person to death, you would. I'll be up in five minutes and I don't want to hear another sound until then.'

The kitchen door bangs. Into the huge silence in the bathroom comes a very small whisper.

'Are we very bad children?'

'Auntie says so.'

Little soapy islands of bubbles drift over the cooling surface of the bathwater.

'I didn't know you could worry a person to death, did you?'

'Shush, we must be quiet.'

The older child fills her sponge with water and squashes it on top of her head, screwing her eyes tight. Water flows down her face.

Aunt has left the door of the dining room ajar.

Quickly, before she notices and kicks it shut, you step to where the thin line of light crosses the hall. You will be able to see them at dinner. It is a circumscribed view: the younger girl opposite, and part of Harry's shoulder nearest, his back to the door, his hand reaching out among the dishes.

Aunt's voice comes: 'Do take more meat, Harry. That wouldn't keep a bird alive.'

The visible little girl looks round surreptitiously to where her sister must be sitting. She gives a little nod that says, 'You see?'

The door snaps shut. You are closed out again, alone in the dark, with your own special hunger.

In the garden, concealment is easily maintained among the dreaming spirits of the flowers. No one here would think that the sudden dip and rustle of leaves means more than the precipitate departure of a bird. The weather is warm enough for the girls to play on the swing. They take it in turns, quietly, decorously. Even here, away from the chastened house and Aunt's long ears, they practise their new, subdued manner.

'You see how Auntie worries all the time about Daddy's health.'

'But we're being good now, all the time...to

help his health.'

'He's all we've got now.'

'Except for Auntie.' The child's voice is gloomy.

'She never used to be so cross.'

'That was before.'

'I wish we'd known before about being bad...'

Visitors have come. Aunt calls the girls from the drawing-room window. They move off towards the house at a sedate pace. The house has grown so gloomy, it is inimical to you, and you cling to your garden haunts, finding peace among your flowers. But still the house and its occupants draw you, entrap you. Voices come clearly from the open window, over the scented daffodils that you planted only last year.

'Such pretty little girls – so like her – yes, I will take sugar, just this once, to be naughty. You have to, now and again...'

'Sit by the window, girls, and mind you don't drop crumbs on the chintz – it's only just washed.'

'Such good children. Such little angels.'

The backs of two well-brushed heads appear just above the level of the windowsill.

'Now, tell us, how has he been?' A discreet voice accompanies the tiny clinks of good teacups being carefully handled.

'He has his work to occupy him – but he is suffering dreadfully. He keeps it all bottled up and it is so bad for him . . .'

'The children . . .'

'He never seems to see them.'

'But you have been a pillar of strength.'

'Only what duty demands . . .'

'What about your work?'

'I know, I know . . . but I can't leave Harry as he is . . . Without someone watching him he'd just fade away.'

The discreet voices murmur on. The two little heads in the window are bowed – the girls are tense, controlled. If only you could waft comfort to them on the breeze that slightly shifts the heavy curtains. The visitors make their elaborate farewells. There are crumbs on the chintz of the window seat.

'Look at that mess. What on earth did you think you were doing? Why can't you be good?' Aunt's anger fills the room. Even the furniture flinches.

'I'm sorry, I'm sorry, I'm sorry,' the girls cry and race from the room.

Aunt comes to stand by the window. Tired, tired, tired she looks.

'I do mean to be kind,' she murmurs to the garden. 'I'm only trying to do my best . . .' Abruptly she reaches up and brings down the sash window with a heavy thump.

*

You come in through the french windows, which have slipped open from their faulty lock. The house has a deserted feel. In the distant kitchen, Aunt is listening to the radio. The girls have hidden themselves away. The rooms, the passageways, the stairs, all are unwatched. You are free to walk through the house at will, revisiting.

At dinner time, when Harry comes home, the girls still have not reappeared.

Aunt is distraught. 'It's all my fault. They've run away. There's been an accident.'

Your heart leaps with joy, because for the first time since he lost you, your husband moves with decision, voluntarily, and not like a machine. 'Calm yourself. Search the house first. They might just be hiding.'

You know where they are because you saw them as you walked the house, and you lingered over their tiny, tucked-away, fast-asleep forms. And so you are smiling now because you know that this new trouble will be smoothed away.

He finds them, cuddled up in a bundle like two sleeping cats, and your heart is singing as you watch the lightening of his face and see that grief is losing its grip on him. Laughing with relief, he gently shakes his daughters awake.

There is an outburst.

'Daddy, Daddy, I'm sorry we're bad. It was us

worried Mummy to death ... it's all our fault she had to die, and now we're bad again ... don't you die ...'

'You poor pets, whatever can have given you such notions?' And then he explains; he explains everything. Comfort comes.

And when comfort comes, it's time for you to go. They won't haunt you any more.